BONE
JACK

BONE JACK

SARA CROWE

Andersen Press • London

First published in 2014 by
Andersen Press Limited
20 Vauxhall Bridge Road
London SW1V 2SA
www.andersenpress.co.uk

2 4 6 8 10 9 7 5 3 1

British Library Cataloguing in Publication Data available.

ISBN: 978 1 783 44005 4

Printed and bound in Great Britain by
Clays Limited, Bungay, Suffolk, NR35 1ED

For my mother and father,
who filled my childhood with stories,
and for Elaine and Joanna who
encouraged me to write my own.
With love.

ONE

Stag's Leap. It felt like the edge of the world, nothing beyond it but a fall of rock, depth and fierce winds.

Ash Tyler looked down.

Today the wind was hot, as dry and rough as sandpaper against his skin. It tore back his hair, made his eyes stream. He leaned into it, testing its strength against his own.

There was still a half a metre or so between him and the edge. He inched forward again. The wind slapped his T-shirt around like a sail.

He'd done this before at least a dozen times. Always his best friend Mark's idea. All the crazy things they'd ever done had been Mark's idea.

Except this time.

Here he was again. Alone, and nothing between him and a hundred metre fall onto splintered rock.

He stretched out his arms like wings, the way Mark always used to. He forced himself to look down. The salt taste of sweat on his lips. The wind singing in his ears.

The ground hurtled up towards him and spun away again.

He braced himself against the wind. For a few moments he felt weightless, free, as if he could soar out over the land, ride the air like a hawk. Fly up, pin himself to the sky, watch the blue Earth spin beneath him.

He was giddy with fear and joy.

He knew that the wind had only to draw its breath to snatch him away, send him flailing down onto the rocks far below.

He tipped his weight forward until only the balls of his feet tethered him to the ground.

Then the wind dropped.

He wobbled. Not much but enough to make fear drill through him. If he fell he'd die, bones shattering, skin ripping against granite, blood on stone.

He tensed. Every sinew wire-taut, every muscle straining.

He hung there for what seemed an age. Then the wind gusted hard again, pushed him upright. He took a step back and then another, sagged down onto the good solid ground.

That had been the closest one yet.

Never again, he told himself. At fifteen, he was too old for these stupid games.

Still trembling from the rush.

Never again.

He rolled onto his back on the parched mountain grass and closed his eyes. The sun was hot on his face. The wind soughed over the mountainside and birds chattered in the gorse. Crickets whirred somewhere close by.

Beyond these tiny sounds stretched a vaster silence. Once it would have been broken by the rough cries of sheep, but there weren't any sheep in the mountains any more. First sickness had weakened them. Then came government men in biohazard suits, the whole area under quarantine, gunshots and terrified bleats shattering the quiet air. Now the sheep were all gone, all dead.

Sometimes Ash imagined he could still smell the stink of blood and burning flesh from the slaughter, the choking disinfectants with which they'd drenched whole farmyards.

The wind dropped again. The air was warm and thick. It clung to his skin like sweat. He sat up, yawned, stretched the tension out of his muscles.

He had a three-mile run home. It was time to get going.

He set off at a steady pace down the path. Soon the rhythms of his body took over. He let his thoughts drift apart and fall away until there was only the beat of his feet, the shunt of his lungs and the hard white sky over raw slopes.

The path ran along a crease in the mountain to a wide flattish shoulder halfway down. Brambles, a collapsed dry-stone wall, and beyond that a cluster of farm buildings where Mark had lived with his family until the bank repossessed it last year.

It had been empty ever since. No one wanted a wind-blasted, run-down hill farm in the aftermath of a foot-and-mouth outbreak.

Ash concentrated on the path. Tried not to look at the farm, not to think about it, not to remember. The memories came anyway, dark and airless. Tom Cullen, Mark's dad, up to his neck in debt, silently watching the carcasses of his slaughtered sheep smoulder in huge pits. His world falling apart.

'We should have seen it coming,' Ash's mum had said afterwards. Eyes full of tears and anger. 'We should have done something.'

But no one had done anything for Tom Cullen.

A battered FOR SALE sign hung on the gate. Beyond it was the yard, an expanse of cracked concrete edged with tall weeds and nettles. The farmhouse windows were boarded up. Around it stood several outbuildings, a rusted tractor resting on its wheel rims, a few empty oil drums.

The old barn, its doors hanging on their hinges, its roof sagging.

When they were kids, he and Mark had bottle-fed lambs in that barn. Turned the hayloft into a den. Once they'd cornered a marauding fox in there, then, awed by its fierce wildness, stepped back and let it run free into the night.

And in that barn, in the dead of night, Tom Cullen had knotted a rope into a noose, slung it over a beam and—

Ash wouldn't let himself think about that.

Not that.

He ran on and didn't look back. Where the path forked, he took the steeper route, a sharp zigzag down-hill between high banks of boulder and gorse.

He came around the shoulder of the mountain and the land opened out before him, greens and greys and purples slashed with fox-red bracken. A wild terrain of deep wide valleys, rough moors, crags.

He liked this route, even though it took him past the Cullen farm. When Dad came home – any day now – they'd come running out here together. They'd camp at one of the mountain lakes, go canoeing and fishing and rock climbing. They'd worked it all out in emails and phone calls.

But lately Dad hadn't been answering his emails or his phone and now he was two days late coming home. Mum was worried. She never said so but Ash knew it and so he worried too. The house phone seemed to ring on and off all day but the callers were never Dad.

'Where the hell are you?' he said out loud to the mountains and the sky. 'Come home, you stupid bastard.'

He ran faster. Only two weeks now until the big race, the annual Stag Chase through the mountains. He'd be the stag boy, the lead runner chased by other boys. And Dad would be back by then. He'd be there. Ash would win. He knew in his heart he would. He was rubbish at most sport but he could run like a stag, run like the wild wind. He'd win and Dad would be waiting at the finish line, brimful with pride.

The whole thing played out like a movie in his mind.

He lengthened his stride, let his body do the thinking, let it make the split-second decisions about footfall and rock and root. Ran through thorn and gorse, over slope, stone, ridged mud, slippery patches of wiry grass. The whisper of the breeze, the scrape and scuttle of loose stones underfoot. A kestrel trembling on the high thermals. The burnt smell of the sun-scorched land.

A bird shot out of the bracken, flew straight at his face. A gaping beak the colour of steel, ragged black wings, claws ripping at his skin. He flung out his hands, felt feather and bone under his fingers. He staggered, lost his footing and crashed down onto a scratchy mattress of heather.

Then the bird was gone. He rolled onto his back and lay there, breathing hard, heart thumping, staring wide-eyed at a darkening sky.

TWO

A few seconds ago the sky had been as pale as the white sun, but now bruised-looking clouds were piling up on each other, a dark avalanche rolling over the land. Still lying on his back, Ash watched it warily. The weather in the mountains could change in the blink of an eye. Last year he'd got caught in a brief, ferocious hailstorm that had come out of nowhere on a clear spring day.

Now it looked as if a rainstorm was going to catch him.

And a tremor in the mountainside, a long low vibration like a roll of thunder except that it couldn't be because it didn't stop, just got louder and closer until the bone-dry ground and the air thrummed with it.

Something coming, something powerful and fast. Not just one thing but many, feet pounding the hard earth; animals or people, Ash couldn't tell which.

Whatever they were, they were coming uphill towards him.

Ash scrambled to his feet, looked around. Nothing. But there was still something coming, the pounding getting louder, closer. He backed away from the path into dense gorse that tore at his bare legs. He couldn't run through that, couldn't get any further away from the path.

He looked for somewhere to hide, but now a stone skittered at the bend below. Behind it came a running boy. He was about Ash's age – fifteen, maybe sixteen – and he was tall and lean like Ash too, wearing rough brown leggings and thin leather boots like some ancient-days character from a movie or a computer game. In the heat haze he seemed spectral and unearthly, a strange shimmering apparition. His hair was sculpted into spikes stiffened with pale mud or clay. More clay caked his face, made a cracked and peeling mask. Above the waist he was naked except for a crude design daubed on his chest, a blood-red stag's head with branching antlers. He stumbled as he ran, lurched and flailed, staggered onwards again. His eyes were wide with terror. His clay face stretched into a silent scream.

The boy was exhausted. Ash could see that straight away. Beyond exhausted. Legs heavy. His head bobbing, breathing in quick wheezy gasps.

But he kept running.

Like he was running for his life.

His gaze met Ash's as he passed but he didn't stop, didn't break his stumbling stride.

Still there was the rumble in the mountainside, stronger now. Ash crouched down low, waited with his breath catching in his throat, hoped whatever was coming up the path wouldn't notice him hiding amidst the bracken and spiky clumps of gorse.

The boy was out of sight now.

Time crawled.

Then more boys appeared further down the mountain. First three or four, then dozens of them streaming into view. As with the first boy, there was something unearthly about them, as if they were tricks of the light rather than flesh and blood. Like him, they wore leggings, masks, thin leather boots strapped at the ankle. But their masks weren't clay. Theirs were ragged things of painted, stiffened sackcloth, masks with eyeholes slashed into them and gaping mouths. Their pace was steady and relentless. They looked as if they could run all day. Soon they'd catch up with the fleeing boy and his race would be over.

Ash knew what they were. Their costumes were wrong, but these were hound boys and this was a Stag

Chase. Except it couldn't be. The Stag Chase was only held once a year and it wasn't for another two weeks and then Ash was going to be the stag boy fleeing the hounds. Not this clay-daubed stranger.

The runners passed Ash as if he wasn't there: ten, twenty, thirty and more of them.

A pack of hounds, running its prey to ground.

The stag boy didn't stand a chance. They'd catch up with him on the ridge, perhaps even sooner.

Ash tensed, about to jump up and help him. Then he stopped. Their unearthliness unnerved him and there were too many of them anyway. And already they were almost out of sight, only the stragglers still visible as the path jackknifed its way up the mountain.

Then the last of them was gone.

Ash stood still, heart hammering, watching the spot where they'd vanished.

A shriek ripped through the silence. Part human, part animal.

The stag boy. It had to be. The hounds must have caught up with him by Stag's Leap.

The blood drained from Ash's face.

Something terrible was happening. He knew it in his bones, as surely as he knew night from day. No one screamed like that except from raw terror. This wasn't just a race. This was dark, savage, murderous. A hunt, with the stag boy as its prey.

He went back to the path, ran a little way along it then scrambled up onto a swell of higher ground to get a better view. He shielded his eyes against the sun and scanned the upper slopes for the boy and the hounds.

They couldn't have got further than that. There hadn't been enough time.

There was no sign of them. Not a sound, not a movement.

They'd gone.

It was as if they'd never been there at all.

The storm clouds had vanished too, sucked back over the horizon. Instead there was the glaring white metal sky again, so bright it hurt his eyes.

A tiny movement further up the mountainside caught his attention. He shielded his eyes and squinted into the sunlight.

There was a girl standing on a boulder, watching him. Her hair was dark and wild. She wore a dress the dusty red of roadside poppies. He recognised her straight away: Callie Cullen, Mark's younger sister.

Relief flooded through him at the sight of someone familiar. Suddenly everything seemed ordinary again.

The impossible Stag Chase gone, the world settling back to its sensible self.

It struck him that Callie must have seen the running boys too, must have seen where they went.

'Callie!' he hollered. 'Hey, Callie! Did you see those runners? Where did they go?'

If she heard him, she didn't answer. She just stood there, watching him, motionless except for the breeze tugging at her dress and hair.

Ash shrugged his shoulders, gave up. Everything that had happened this morning was too weird for him. All he wanted now was to be back at home, in his own room where things made sense and he could shut the door, lose himself in a computer game, keep the world at arm's length. And soon Dad would be home, maybe even today, and everything would be OK.

Nothing else mattered.

He set off at an unsteady trot, still shaky with adrenalin. His legs sloshed around as if they were full of water.

Heat shimmered on the mountainside, split the air, played tricks on his eyes. Faraway things seemed close, close things seemed further than they really were. And shadows raced alongside him, like the shadows of scudding clouds. Except there weren't any clouds, not any more, just the white-hot sky stretching from horizon to horizon.

The shadows spooked him. He didn't look back. Instead he ran harder, faster, and he didn't stop until he reached home.

THREE

Mum was pottering around in the garden when he got back. Wearing her frayed straw hat, harvesting sweetcorn from plants as tall, slender and dishevelled-looking as she was. He waved at her through the kitchen window, watched her for a while.

Things getting back to normal, bit by bit. Just Dad missing.

He poured two glasses of orange juice and took them out into the garden.

Mum had been busy. A basket heaped with ears of sweetcorn stood at her feet.

'Impressive crop, Mum,' said Ash.

'It's about the only one that's done well in this drought. So we'll be having sweetcorn with every meal for the next month.' She pushed a loose strand of her pale hair back under her hat and smiled at him.

'Including breakfast.'

Ash pulled a face. 'Bacon, eggs and sweetcorn? Gross. What's wrong with the sweetcorn that comes in tins, anyway?'

'And what's wrong with eating pizza every day?' She laughed and tidied his wind-wilded hair, the way she used to when he was small. He groaned a protest but he didn't pull away.

She let him go. She sipped her juice, set the glass down next to the basket and twisted off another ear of corn. 'Did you have a good run?'

Ash hesitated. He wanted to tell her about the bird flying into his face, about the stag boy being hunted down, how the running boys seemed to vanish into thin air, the freaky storm clouds, the shadows that had chased him. But when the words formed in his mind, it all sounded creepy and unreal, a mad dream best kept to himself.

She had enough to worry about anyway, with Dad still not back.

'Yeah, it wasn't bad,' he said. 'I went up to Stag's Leap. I saw Callie Cullen up there.'

'Callie?' Mum stopped breaking the corn ears from their stalks and gave him her full attention. 'Was Mark with her?'

'No. It was just her.'

'What in the world was she doing out there by herself? Did you talk to her?'

'Yeah, but she wouldn't talk to me.'

'Why ever not?' said Mum. 'Those poor kids. You and Mark used to be such good friends. I wish you'd try again with him.'

'I tried lots of times.' His face grew hot. It wasn't exactly a lie – he had made an effort after Mark's dad hanged himself. But bad things seemed to collect around Mark after his dad died. Dark and violent things. When Mark pushed him away, Ash let himself be pushed and then time passed and things got awkward. These days they scarcely saw each other.

He couldn't explain all that to Mum. She wouldn't get it. She'd remind him that Mark had been his best friend, tell him not to be so superstitious and silly. There'd be disappointment in her eyes, in her voice.

He couldn't stand that.

He cleared his throat and changed the subject. 'Has Dad called yet?'

Stupid question. If he had called, she'd have told him by now.

'Not yet,' said Mum. Her voice suddenly sounded too cheerful. 'I'm sure he'll be home soon though.'

Ash nodded and drained his glass of juice. 'Right. I'll go and have a shower.'

'Good idea,' said Mum. 'I didn't want to mention it but...'

'Yeah, I'm all sweaty and I stink. I know, Mum.'

He stood in the shower for a long time, letting the hot water sluice away the sweat and dust from his run. Then he towelled himself dry, went up to his bedroom in the attic and put on fresh clothes.

Through the open bedroom window, he heard the garden gate shriek on its hinges.

It was probably just the postman, he told himself. But his heart leaped anyway and he rushed to the window.

It wasn't the postman.

It was Dad.

FOUR

Dad was standing in the driveway, just inside the gate. He looked the way Ash remembered: tall, broad-shouldered, tough as teak. His jaw was shadowed with stubble. He was dressed in his civvies and his dark hair was messy, despite the regulation army cut, but he still looked a soldier through and through.

Captain Stephen Tyler, home from war.

Then Dad walked out onto the lawn and it all started to fall apart. He looked loose somehow, as if his bones weren't properly connected. Dragging his feet, swaying, stumbling.

Like a puppet with its strings cut.

Ash watched and a tiny knife of anxiety twisted inside him.

In the middle of the lawn, Dad stopped. He stared at the house as if it was somewhere he remembered from a dream. Then he looked straight up at the open window where Ash was.

Ash stuck out his head. 'Dad! Hey, Dad!'

Dad just went on staring, as if Ash was a stranger to him. No smile, no wave, not even a flicker of recognition.

Ash flinched as if he'd been slapped across the face.

Dad took another step, lurched sideways, almost fell.

Drunk, thought Ash. Or something else wrong, something worse.

Anxiety cut through him again.

Mum came around the side of the house. She was still wearing her old straw hat. She stopped for a long moment, watching Dad. He hadn't noticed her. He was still staring up at the house as if he'd never seen it before. She called out to him, her voice soft and low and so full of love that Ash suddenly felt afraid for her.

Dad looked across at her. He smiled weirdly, then a sob broke from him and he buckled, seemed about to crumple to his knees on the grass. Then Mum was running towards him and she caught him in her arms, held him close, held him up.

Ash turned away, embarrassed. They didn't seem like his parents any more. Instead they were like two strangers caught in the middle of something huge and terrible, something he didn't understand, didn't want to see.

He lay on his bed, stared at the ceiling.

A door slammed downstairs. He closed his eyes. A blood-red glare behind his eyelids, and circling specks of black that opened dark wings and flapped away like carrion crows over a battlefield.

He curled up into a ball, rocked himself for a while, opened his eyes again.

However much he wanted to, he couldn't stay up here for ever. Sunshine outside, Dad downstairs. Mum. The Stag Chase only a fortnight away. Everything waiting for him. So he got up, went down there.

They were sitting at the kitchen table, mugs of tea in front of them. Typical, Ash thought. Everything falling apart and Mum had made a pot of tea.

Dad looked exhausted. Bruises under his eyes, his skin too thin and too tight, greyish under his desert tan. He glanced at Ash and then away again.

He looked ill. Injured, maybe, Ash thought. But the army would have told them if Dad had been injured, so not that. It wasn't just drunkenness though. He'd seen Dad drunk before. Not often, but enough to know that this was different in some dark, deeper way that he didn't understand.

'Your dad's home,' said Mum. As if Dad wasn't sitting right next to her.

'I know,' said Ash. He tried to smile, to make a joke of it. 'I can see him.'

He pulled out a chair. The chair legs screeched across the lino and Dad winced.

Silence except for the tick of the wall clock.

Mum shot him a look. He knew what she wanted him to do. He was supposed to talk to Dad, act as if everything was normal so they could all pretend it really was, that Dad was his old self and that everything would be wonderful now he was home.

That was how it was supposed to be when your dad came back after months away at war. Family time. Hugs and laughter and love. A celebration.

The silence filled the room. Then Dad's eyes half closed and he slumped a bit in his chair, almost slid off it onto the floor, grabbed the edge of the table to save himself. Tea slopped out of the mugs.

'He's drunk,' said Ash. The words punched out like machine-gun fire before he could stop them. 'He stinks of beer.'

'That's enough, Ash,' said Mum sharply. 'You're not helping.'

He looked at her, looked at Dad. Tears burned behind his eyes.

'I'm tired,' said Dad, to no one in particular. The

words slurring together. 'If you don't mind, I need to sleep now.'

He stood up. So did Mum.

'No!' said Dad. Voice cracking out like a whip. Mum looked shocked. 'Sorry,' he said. 'I'm sorry. I just need some sleep. I'll be all right tomorrow.'

He moved into the spare room with his rucksack, as if he was a guest.

And Ash knew he wouldn't be all right tomorrow.

FIVE

Morning, and the distant mountains looked like a watercolour dissolving in rain, colours running together. But it was the heat haze that made the air shiver and blur, not rain. There hadn't been any rain for almost two months. The grass was brittle and burned golden brown and the streams had shrunk to sluggish trickles that were more mud than water. Everything was tired, wilting, dusty, and Ash felt the same way, felt a hundred years old, all his strength and energy leached out.

He had a shopping list and a folded ten-pound note in his pocket. He knew the shopping was just Mum's excuse to get him out of the house but he didn't care. It was a relief to get out for a while, not to be at home with Dad in such a mess, not to be saying stupid angry things like he had yesterday. He was better off out of it.

He headed past the Old Rec, towards the row of little shops on the other side of the main street.

Then he saw her out on the Rec, sitting on one of the swings. Callie Cullen, barefoot and still wearing the dusty red dress he'd seen her in yesterday. Her serious grey eyes watched him. He got the feeling she'd been waiting for him. But she couldn't have been. She couldn't have known Mum would send him out to the shops.

He went over and sat on the swing next to hers. He breathed in the smells of hot tarmac, rubber, old bubble gum. Playground smells.

'I saw you yesterday,' he said. 'Out in the mountains, up by Stag's Leap.'

'So what?'

The edge of dislike in her voice shocked him. They'd never been friends exactly, but she'd always been there, at the edge of his life, a quiet, serious girl with a slow shy smile. He'd always thought she liked him well enough, as much as he'd thought about her at all. Now she sounded like she almost hated him.

He bit his lip, looked away. After a while he said, 'Did you see anyone else out there?'

'Like who?'

'Like runners,' he said. 'Lots of them. Hound boys.'

'No, I didn't see anyone.'

'You must have seen them. They ran up the path to the top of the ridge. They must have run right past you.'

'The Stag Chase isn't for another two weeks.'

'I know that.'

'They can't have been hound boys then. Anyway, I didn't see them. I didn't see anyone.'

She was lying. He was sure of it. There was no way she could have missed the runners.

'You're lying,' he said.

He expected her to get angry and deny it but she didn't. She just gave him a look that said she didn't really care what he thought.

Somehow that was worse. It meant maybe she was telling the truth and he was the only one who had seen the runners. And if he was the only one who'd seen them, then maybe he'd imagined them, maybe they'd never been there at all.

Seeing things, mirages, like people saw in deserts. Tricks of the light. Or of the mind.

He tilted his weight a little. The swing moved. His feet scraped across the safety surface.

'I heard Mark moved in with your grandpa,' he said.

A guarded look. 'Yeah, we stay there sometimes.'

'Only sometimes? Where do you stay the rest of the time?'

She shrugged, gazed off into the distance. 'Here and there.'

'How's Mark doing?'

'What do you care?'

That was it, Ash knew. The reason for the anger that kept coming back into her voice. She thought he'd betrayed Mark, abandoned him when Mark needed him the most. As far as Callie was concerned, that made him the enemy.

He didn't blame her for feeling that way.

'I couldn't...' he said. Stumbling over the words. 'Everything changed after your dad died. Mark changed. He was like a stranger. I didn't know what to do. I didn't know what to say to him.'

'What did you expect?' said Callie. 'We'd already lost our mum, then Dad killed himself. We lost the farm. Our home. We lost everything. After that Mark wouldn't talk to anyone for a long time, not even to grandpa or me. He clammed up and got strange and crazy.' She looked straight at Ash. 'But he was still Mark.'

'I'm sorry.'

'Sorry's no use. It's just a word you say to make yourself feel better.'

'I don't feel better.'

'You don't deserve to. You were supposed to be his best mate, but you just gave up on him.'

'I'm sorry,' he said again.

'He wants to see you,' said Callie. 'That's why I'm here. I was going to go on up to your house later.'

'What does he want?'

'I don't know. He's the one who wants to see you, not me.'

'When?'

'Tomorrow night. It has to be tomorrow night.'

'I can't come tomorrow.' Not when Dad had only been home a day, he thought. But he couldn't tell Callie that, couldn't tell her that his dad had come home safe from war when her own dad was dead.

'You're just the same,' she said. 'Useless.'

'Maybe next week. I can't get to your grandpa's house tomorrow. Mum's busy so I can't get a lift.' Immediately he reddened at the lie. It was only a few miles to Coldbrook, where Grandpa Cullen lived. Callie knew as well as he did that it would take him less than half an hour on his bike.

'He's not staying at Grandpa's,' she said. 'He's hardly ever there.'

'I can't make it,' he said. 'Why does it have to be

tomorrow, anyway?'

'Because that's when he wants to see you,' she said. 'Because next week might be too late.'

'Too late for what?'

'It has to be tomorrow night,' she said again, looking away. 'That's what Mark said.'

'I can't. There's stuff going on at home. Mum needs me there.'

'Your dad's back,' she said. 'I know about that. You don't have to lie.'

He stared at her, shocked. 'How do you know he's back?'

'You know what it's like around here,' she said. 'Everyone knows everyone else's business.'

'Seriously, who told you?'

'Relax. No one told me. I saw the taxi drop him off at the top of your lane yesterday. Then he walked towards your house. He looked in a bad way.'

'Drunk,' said Ash. 'He was drunk.'

'He probably had his reasons.'

'I don't know. Maybe he did. I don't know what's wrong with him. He's a mess.'

She shot him a strange look and this time he glowered back at her. He'd had enough of her judging him all the time, first about Mark and now about Dad. So self-righteous. So sure that he was a waste of space.

'Go on then,' he said. 'What reasons? Tell me.'

'You're an idiot, Ash Tyler.'

'Tell me.'

'Your dad just got back from a war.' She spoke slowly, as if she was explaining something very simple to someone very stupid. 'A war. He must have seen terrible things. He must have been shot at, seen bombs going off. He must have seen people getting killed. Blood and guts. His own men, and enemy fighters, and ordinary people who just got in the way. Old people. Women. Kids.'

The muscles in Ash's jaw were so tense they ached.

'Look up "shell shock" on the internet when you get home,' said Callie. 'Look up "survivor guilt" and "post-traumatic stress disorder".'

'How come you know it all?'

'We did it at school last year. The First World War. A lot of soldiers in the trenches got shell shock.'

'Right,' he said, tight-lipped.

'I'll wait for you at the Monks Bridge at nine tomorrow night,' she said. 'If you come, I'll take you to Mark. If you don't, he'll never ask you again.'

'I'll try,' he said. 'It depends.'

He remembered the shopping list in his pocket and

stood up. The swing creaked on its chains, knocked against the backs of his legs.

She called after him as he walked away. 'Those runners,' she said, 'the hound boys you said you saw – you should ask Mark about them.'

'Why? What's he got to do with them?'

'He knows everything that goes on in the mountains. Ask him.'

Ash shrugged. She was probably only saying it to get him to meet her tomorrow night.

He crossed the road to the little grocery shop. There was a poster in the window, a stylised stag's head in blood-red paint against a black background. 'Share in the excitement of Thornditch's historic Stag Chase', the poster said. A thrill ran through him. For a moment, nothing else mattered, not Dad, not Mark. Just that he was the stag boy, that he'd won the trials, beaten all the other boys. All eyes would be on him at the start of the race. His heart quickened at the thought of it. He'd run and he'd win and he'd be a hero for the first time in his life.

He went inside the shop, wandered along narrow strips of ancient chequered lino between high walls of shelving stacked with tinned soup, boxes of breakfast cereal, loo rolls. The hum of the refrigerator at the back of the shop. Reedy voices on the radio that old Mr Linnet listened to as he sat on his chair behind the wooden counter with its scratchcard display and trays of sherbet flying saucers. Everything exactly the same as it had been ever since Ash could remember.

Today it felt like the still point at the centre of a chaotic universe.

He took his time gathering the items on Mum's shopping list: eggs, bread, milk.

'Ready for the Stag Chase?' said Mr Linnet.

'Yeah, I think so.'

'I remember when your dad was the stag boy. Must be twenty years ago now. There was a drought that year too, as I recall. Not half as bad as this one, mind. How is your dad, anyway?'

'He's all right. He's home. Got back yesterday.'

'He'll be coming to watch you run then. He must be very proud of you.'

'Yeah, I suppose so.'

As he watched Mr Linnet tot up the bill, the hairs on the back of his neck prickled as if there was something out there, in the hard sunlight outside. Something watching, waiting.

He looked up.

Five faces at the window, faces as pale and blank as

masks. Boys he recognised from school, sixth-formers from Coldbrook.

He stared back at them, unnerved.

'Four pounds and fifty-two pence, please,' said Mr Linnet.

Ash fumbled in his pockets for Mum's tenner. When he looked up again, the boys were gone. Only a movement across the street, a flap of black as if the breeze had caught the tail of someone's coat as they swung a corner. Then there was nothing except a rook shaking out its feathers on a wall before winging away into the pale sky.

SIX

At lunchtime Mum made lasagne and loaded a tray for Dad.

'He hasn't eaten anything since he got back,' she said. 'Not so much as a bite.'

'I'll take it up to him if you want,' said Ash.

She hesitated.

'It'll be OK, Mum. Come on, I'll do it.'

He knocked before he went into Dad's room. There was no answer but he went in anyway. It was night-dark in there, the heavy curtains pulled so tight that not even a thread of light showed. The air smelled of sweat and unwashed clothes.

'Dad, I can't see anything. I'm going to put the light on, OK?'

A grunt from across the room.

Ash flicked the switch.

Dad was on the hard single bed, adrift among all the random bits of furniture and junk stored here because they didn't fit anywhere else. He was lying on his side, facing the door, the sheet pulled up to his ears. His rucksack was on the floor nearby, clothes spilling out of it.

Ash put down the tray on a small table and dragged it across to the bed.

'Mum made lunch for you. Lasagne.'

Dad's eyes opened a crack. 'Thanks. Just leave it there.'

'You getting up?'

'In a while.'

'You'll feel better if you get up.' Ash hovered by the bed. He trawled his mind for something more to say. 'You could come out running with me tomorrow, Dad. If you want.'

'Not tomorrow. Maybe next week.'

Next week. Or never. Then he remembered. He hadn't told Dad yet that he'd entered the Stag Chase, that he'd won the trials and so he'd be the stag boy in this year's race. It was supposed to be a surprise, his great gift to Dad on his homecoming.

Some gift.

He should tell him now, get it over with.

But he couldn't. The timing was all wrong. In the state

he was in, Dad would barely even register the news. And it had to be big, it had to be special.

Ash drew a deep slow breath, exhaled again. 'OK,' he said. 'Next week then.'

'Maybe.'

'Right. Maybe. Do you want me to leave the light on?'

'No. Turn it off. I want to sleep.'

Ash stood there for a few moments. He felt useless, helpless. An abyss yawning between him and Dad and all he could think of was the lasagne congealing, the salad wilting, the bread roll going dry and hard. He told himself it didn't matter. It was just food.

But somehow it did matter.

'Mum made it for you,' he said. 'Her special lasagne. It's what you always want when you get home, better than all that army food. Mum says you haven't eaten anything since you got back. You need to eat, Dad.'

'I will eat.'

'You won't. You'll leave it and it'll get disgusting.'

'I said I'll eat it,' said Dad. Pulling the sheet up over his head, mumbling through the cotton. 'I'll eat it when you've gone.'

Ash started to leave.

'I'll be all right tomorrow,' said Dad.

'Yeah,' said Ash. 'You said that yesterday.'

He switched off the light, closed the door behind him and went up to his bedroom.

He sat at his desk, staring at the photographs pinned to the corkboard above it. Dad on one of the climbing expeditions he used to go on with his army mates when he was younger. Up on some mountain, blue sky beyond. Dad was weather-burned, squinting into the sun, smiling like he didn't have a care in the world.

More than anything, he wanted the Dad in the photograph back – strong and capable, always up for adventure.

But that Dad was gone. Maybe for ever.

His gaze travelled over the other pictures on the corkboard. A print of a leaping wolf he'd cut from a magazine; an eerie photograph of a fox on a misty moonlit night; a shot of Stag's Leap, raw and mysterious under a stormy sky. An old picture of Mark, taken at the farm a couple of years ago. They'd been downhilling that day, shredding their bikes along the dirt track on Tolley Carn. Mark was mud-spattered and grinning, eyes full of light and laughter.

It seemed a lifetime ago.

Ash looked away. He booted up the laptop and opened the web browser.

He typed 'shell shock' into the search engine.

Hundreds of hits came up: medical sites, psychology sites, sites about the First and Second World Wars, Vietnam, the Falklands, Afghanistan, Iraq. Help groups for veterans. Videos.

He clicked on a video link. Grainy black-and-white film from a century ago, soldiers who'd fought in the trenches and survived to come home. Men who shook and twitched, wide-eyed with terror, as if the war was still raging around them and shrapnel might rip through flesh and bone at any moment.

A soldier hiding his face, trying to get away from the camera, trotting jerkily in frightened circles.

Like a beaten dog.

Ash couldn't watch any more. He slammed the laptop shut, sat staring at the wall, seeing nothing.

Slowly he came back to himself. His eyes focused on a small picture of the Stag Chase twenty years ago, the year Dad had been the stag boy. There he was, outside the Huntsman Inn in Thornditch, wearing the ancient antler headdress that the stag boy paraded in if he won his race. He looked uncomfortable, stiffly posed, his expression solemn instead of triumphant.

Dad must have been about seventeen back then. Two years older than Ash was now. He was powerfully built even at that age. Not a distance runner's physique like

Ash's. Ash didn't look much like him at all. He had Mum's fair hair and her slender, bony frame. He wasn't strong like Dad, wasn't a fighter. But his eyes were like Dad's, so people said. Blue and intense.

He took the photograph down from the corkboard and looked at it more closely. There were hound boys in the background, prowling predatory youths still acting out their roles even after the race was over.

They seemed more hound than boy.

One of them stood apart from the others. He wore his mask pushed back over the top of his head. Tom Cullen, Mark and Callie's dad. He was smiling, his face not yet set into the stern lines that Ash remembered.

Ash pinned the photograph back onto the corkboard.

Too much thinking.

He needed to do something, anything except sit there with his mind spinning. He stood, scooped up his dirty running gear to dump it in the laundry basket.

Something fell to the floor.

It was a feather, about six inches long. Black, with a metallic purple sheen that shimmered in the light like oil on water. He remembered the bird that had flown into him on the mountain path. The dry brittle touch of its hollow bones, its inky feathers. One of those feathers must have snagged on his clothing.

And now it was here, in his bedroom, a fragment of darkness he'd accidentally brought back with him. He stared at it so long that it started to lose its shape, blurring at the edges, leaking shadow that joined up with other shadows, spreading like a dense black mist across the floor.

He had to get rid of it. But that meant he'd have to go closer to it, touch it, hold it. The thought made his skin crawl. He took a step towards it, felt a dark pull, a sickening depth opening before him. Another step, and another. He stopped and bent down. Turned his face away from it, half closed his eyes. Held his breath. His fingertips brushed over the carpet, over the feather. He forced himself to pick it up.

His head swam. He lurched and swayed, slammed his hand down on the floor to balance himself. He closed his eyes tight until the giddiness subsided.

The room was itself again. The feather just a feather.

And yet it wasn't just a feather. It meant something. It had some dark power. He'd felt it. He didn't understand it, not yet, but it had been real.

There was no way he wanted the thing in his bedroom or even in the house. He could drop it out of the window. He imagined it lying down there among the flowers and weeds, seeping evil. Still too close.

It had to be miles away.

He put it in his backpack.

He'd get rid of it tomorrow, somewhere far from the house.

SEVEN

The next night, Callie was waiting for him at the Monks Bridge, just as she'd promised. The red dress gone, replaced with combat trousers and a fleece that looked three sizes too big for her. There was no sign of Mark. A ghostly half-moon sat low above the trees. Bats flitted through the smoky blue dusk, quick blinks of shadow. Below the bridge the little river slid along, as sleek and brown as an otter.

'Well, I'm here,' said Ash. 'Where's Mark?'

'Somewhere,' she said. Watched him with eyes as silver as the moonlight. 'I'll take you to him. Come on.'

'Wait,' he said. 'There's something I have to do first.'

He took the feather out of his backpack. In the half-light, it looked like nothing, just an ordinary black feather, its power over him nothing but a memory now.

He leaned over the side of the bridge and dropped it.

It was gone in an instant, borne away by the fast water below.

'OK,' he said. 'We can go now.'

'What was that?' said Callie.

'Just a feather.'

She shot him a sideways look. 'A feather?'

'It's not important,' he said. 'A bird flew into me. One of its feathers must have stuck to me.'

'I saw you get it out of your backpack. You brought it all the way out here just so you could drop it in the river?'

He shrugged as if it was no big deal. 'Yeah. Are you taking me to see Mark or what?'

'This way,' she said, and set off.

They were half a mile out of the village on a lane that bucked and twisted along the mountainside, linking farmhouses. 'We'll have to go cross-country part of the way,' said Callie.

'Where to?'

'It doesn't have a name.'

'It must have. Everywhere has a name.'

'If it does, I don't know it. It's just a wood.' She pointed away into the darkening twilight. 'Over there.'

'How far is it?'

'Not far.'

They trudged along in silence. Again he felt her disapproval of him, the cold force of her rage.

'It must have been hard for you when your dad died,' he said. Immediately he cringed inside at his own words. Lately almost everything that came out of his mouth sounded idiotic.

'Look,' she said, 'I don't want to talk about that stuff. I'm taking you to Mark, that's all, because he wants to talk to you. And you used to be his best friend so maybe you can help him, but probably you can't. Anyway, he wants to see you and that's the only reason I'm here with you.'

'Fine,' he muttered, annoyed with her again.

They left the lane, climbed over a stile in thickening gloom. As Ash's eyes adapted to the darkness, he could make out a faint path around the edge of the field. An untidy hedge to his left. Long grass spiked with thistles to his right.

Beyond the field, woodland stretched like a dark wound around the foot of the mountain.

They paused just before the tree line. A twig snapped close by. A low bough jerked and shook its leaves. Ash stared into the gloom, his heart jumping. 'What was that?'

'Just the wild.'

He looked at Callie. She seemed like a wild creature herself, as silent and secret as a fox slipping through the night.

He smelled wood smoke and now, as the path took them on through the trees, he saw firelight flicker deep in the clotted shadows.

Callie stopped. 'That's Mark's campfire over there,' she said. 'He'll be around there somewhere.'

'Aren't you coming with me?'

She shook her head. 'He wants to talk to you, not me. Go on.'

He watched her go, her slight figure becoming a shadow that melted away into the night until at last it swallowed her and he was alone.

Except for Mark.

He went deeper into the woods, then stopped in his tracks, his breath catching in his throat. A gaunt white face stared down at him, long and bony, its eyes hollow with night.

Beyond it, other faces gleamed in the dark, a dozen or more of them.

He started to back away. Then he realised what they were. Skulls, sheep skulls. Some wedged in the forks of branches, others stuck up on sticks driven into the ground or turning slowly at the ends of strings tied around boughs. Three dead rooks, feet bound together, swinging from a branch. Feathers blacker than the fire-cut dark, black as the feather he'd found in his bedroom.

And behind the rooks and the skulls, monstrous shadows shifted among the trees, a dozen or more of them. Figures in masks, distorted and weird, throwing out long limbs, leaping, plunging, twisting.

Freaky shadow people dancing like crazed shamans around the fire.

Mark had company.

Ash dropped into a crouch behind a tree and watched them dance. They were quick and agile, soaring up, spinning, tangling, tearing apart, re-forming and sinking to the ground only to leap up again.

His heart thumped so loudly he was sure they'd hear it.

Fear ran through him. The dancing boys seemed more than human and somehow less at the same time. Half boy and half beast, as airy as wraiths, as dark as the night.

And Mark was in there with them.

They're just shadows thrown by hound boys in fancy dress, Ash told himself. That's all. Maybe this was just a game, the usual ritual in the run-up to the Chase, when the hound boys tormented the stag boy and tried to unnerve him to give the race a dangerous edge.

Or maybe it was something else.

But he was here now. Callie had brought him and Mark was expecting him. He couldn't get out of it. He'd look like a coward and an idiot if he ran away or crouched behind a tree all night.

He drew a deep breath to steady his nerves, then stood up and walked out into the clearing.

His arrival seemed to shatter a spell. The shadowy boys spun away into the night. They didn't go far though, he was sure of that. He couldn't see them any more but he sensed them still out there, lurking among the trees, beyond the circle of firelight. Watching him.

Now they were gone, he saw Mark. He was standing in front of the fire, facing it. He was dressed in loose, torn trousers and nothing else. His hair was matted and spiked with pale clay, his body caked with it.

Ash had seen that look before, on the stag boy running in the mountains.

'Mark,' he said, walking towards the fire. 'Hey, Mark. It's me. Ash. Callie brought me. She said you wanted to talk to me.'

Mark turned. His face was a cracked clay mask. There were charcoal smudges around his eyes. Skull-faced, death-faced. His grin flashed bright and fierce in the firelight. 'Ash,' he said. 'You came then. I thought you'd chicken out.'

'Yeah,' said Ash. 'I nearly did.'

Mark nodded. His gaze slid away towards the trees on the other side of the fire.

'What's with the zombie look?' said Ash.

Mark looked at him again. He raised his arms straight out in front of him, slackened his jaw, took a few stiff-legged steps towards Ash. 'Mwuuuuh! I smell fresh meat. Human meat. Mwuuuuh!'

Ash laughed. 'You're still an idiot,' he said. 'Where have the others gone? The boys who were dancing around the fire?'

Mark dropped his arms back down to his sides. 'Dancing boys?'

'Yeah, those boys who were leaping around the fire a minute ago. All dressed up in hound costumes. Looked like that, anyway. Then they ran off when I got here. Who were they? Why did they run off like that?'

Mark shrugged and cocked his head. 'You're the one who saw them. You tell me.'

'Stop playing mind games with me,' said Ash. 'You got Callie to bring me out here so you could talk to me. I know what I saw.'

'You know what you saw,' said Mark. 'Except you don't know, do you? You're the stag boy, but you don't even know what it means, not really. You don't know anything about the Stag Chase. You don't know its history. You're not fit to be the stag boy.'

'Tell me then,' said Ash. 'You seem to know it all.'

Abruptly Mark's eyes hardened and his mocking smile twisted into a snarl. He took three long, running leaps at Ash, flung out his fist, caught Ash a hammer blow on the jaw. Ash staggered backwards, his legs collapsing under him. His mouth flooded with the thin taste of metal. He gagged and spat blood.

Mark loomed over him. 'This isn't a game,' he said.

'What isn't a game?' said Ash. 'I don't know what the hell you're talking about.'

He was on all fours on the forest floor, the dry mulch of last year's leaf-fall under him. His mouth felt thick and raw. His voice sounded as if it was rolling over pebbles.

'You're the stag boy,' said Mark. 'Do you think it's just about winning a race?'

'Yeah,' said Ash. 'I think it's just about winning a race. Like it was last year and every year before that.'

'You're half right,' said Mark. Softer now, serious. 'Mostly it's just about winning a race. These days,

49

anyway. But sometimes it isn't. Sometimes it's about a lot more than that. Sometimes it's about the old ways. About life and death and the past and the land. It's about making wrong things right again.'

'You're crazy,' said Ash.

Mark crouched in front of him and cuffed him on the shoulder. 'Sorry I hit you,' he said. 'You had it coming though.'

'Did I?'

'Yeah, you did,' said Mark. Still smiling, but the vicious edge creeping back into his voice. 'My dad died. Remember that? He was all we had, Callie and me. Then he died and you couldn't be seen for dust. My best mate. You just abandoned me.'

'It wasn't like that.'

'Don't lie to me, Ash. It was exactly like that.'

'I didn't know what to do.'

'So you ran away.'

'Yeah. I suppose so.'

'And now your dad's come back. My dad died but yours came back. Do you think that's fair?'

'Callie told you about Dad coming home?'

'Of course she told me. She's my sister. She's loyal, that one. Not like you. Do you think it's right, that my dad died and yours came home? You're useless and a coward but your dad is fine. And I didn't do anything wrong but mine died. Is that fair?'

'It's not my fault that your dad killed himself.'

'I didn't say it was your fault. I asked you if you think it's fair.'

'No,' said Ash softly. 'I don't think it's fair.'

'See, I've got to make it right again. Whatever it takes, however hard it is.'

'Is this why you got Callie to bring me out here? So you could beat me up and blame me for everything?'

Mark's eyes glittered in the firelight. 'No,' he said. 'That's not why.' Then his mood seemed to change again. He helped Ash to his feet, draped his arm across Ash's shoulders. 'Do you want some water?'

Uneasy, Ash nodded. Mark seemed capable of anything, laughing one minute, punching him the next. Now this.

'Here.' Mark handed him a bottle. Ash rinsed blood from his mouth, spat, rinsed again.

'Are you hungry?'

'A bit.'

'Good.' Mark picked up a charred length of stick, crouched by the fire. He raked the stick through the embers and rolled out a heavy lump wrapped in blackened tinfoil. 'Venison. Road kill.'

'Road kill?'

'Yeah. Don't worry, it's fresh, not some maggoty old carcass. A stag hit by a car this morning along the valley road. Its blood was still wet and warm when I found it.'

They squatted on their heels, tearing with their teeth at the meat, washing it down with bottled water, sucking their greasy fingers. Ash's jaw ached where Mark had punched him, but at least the strong smoky flavour of the venison took away the taste of blood. For a while, everything seemed almost normal again, the way things were when they were still kids, camping out on summer nights.

When they'd finished eating, Mark tossed the gnawed bones among the trees. 'For the foxes,' he said. 'Out here, if you take something then you have to give something back.'

Ash stared into the flames, into the glowing red heart of the fire. 'Have you been living out here by yourself all summer?' he said.

'Most of the time, yeah.'

'Living on road kill,' said Ash. 'And rooks.'

'I don't eat the rooks.' Mark laughed. 'And it's not just road kill. I hunt and fish too. There's rabbit and wood pigeon and berries and trout and mushrooms. My dad taught me how to live off the land. There's all sorts of stuff to eat, if you know where to look.'

'Like when we used to go camping when we were kids.'

'Yeah,' said Mark. 'A bit like that, except we used to take soggy cheese-and-tomato sandwiches with us and a flask of hot chocolate. We were just kids messing around then. Things are different now.'

'I'm sorry about your dad,' said Ash. 'I'm sorry I wasn't around much afterwards. I should have—'

'Yeah, you should have. But you didn't. When the going got tough, you ran for the hills. You literally ran for the hills. Ran and kept running.'

'I tried to talk to you.'

'Not hard enough.'

'I know. I'm sorry.' That word again. He was sick of saying it but it kept coming out. 'I wish things were still the way they used to be.'

Mark gave a short laugh, sharp as a fox yelp. 'Things are what they are,' he said. 'And they're nothing like the way they used to be.'

'I'll make it right somehow.'

'My dad's dead. We've lost the farm. How will you make that right?'

'That's not what I meant. Of course I can't make that right.'

SARA CROWE

'No, you can't. Only one thing can make that right.'

'What then?'

'The death of the stag boy.'

Ash stared at him. 'What do you mean?'

'The stag boy has to die. It's the only way to put things right. Life for life.'

Ash shifted a little, uneasy. He thought about the spectral stag boy he'd seen running in the mountains, the hound boys hungering along his trail. That terrible scream.

'The land's sick,' said Mark. 'The sickness killed all the sheep. Killed my dad. Now there's drought, crops all withered in the fields in the valleys, and the old ways are coming back. The land needs blood. The stag boy's blood. That's the way it used to be, a sacrifice to the land in a time of want. Well, it's a time of want again, isn't it? The land is dying and there are ghosts rising from its bones, ghosts that kill.'

'Ghost stories. No one believes that stuff, not really.'

'I believe it,' said Mark. 'More than that. I know it's true. That's why I asked Callie to bring you here, so I could tell you to pull out of the Stag Chase.'

'You want me to pull out of the race because of some stupid story about ghosts and the old ways?' said Ash.

Mark bared his teeth, a smile or a snarl. 'It's just a race. It's not that big a deal.'

'It's a big deal to me. No way I'm going to pull out.'

'Then you'll die,' said Mark.

'I'm not going to die. No one's going to die.'

Ash gazed into the fire. A charred branch, bowed like the scorched rib of a giant beast, collapsed into the flames. Firefly sparks and flakes of snowy ash eddied skywards. Ash breathed in a lungful of smoke and started to cough. Then he froze, stifling his coughs with his hands.

Someone was watching them.

EIGHT

Ash only caught a glimpse of him. A face among the shadows, a dark bulk. Then the man turned away and was gone, vanished into the night.

'There's someone here,' said Ash. He pointed towards where the man had stood. 'Over there, in the trees. A man.'

Mark glanced across. 'No one there now.'

'He was there. I saw him.'

'What did he look like?'

Ash shrugged. 'Big. Wearing dark clothes, I think.'

'Was he wearing a hat?'

'I don't know. Maybe.'

'Bone Jack,' muttered Mark. Scowling, angry again.

'Who?'

'The wild man, the soul-taker.'

'The what?'

'It's Bone Jack who guards the boundary between the living and the dead out here. He keeps each in its place and he takes lives as he sees fit. My dad. The road-kill stag. It makes no difference to him. It could be you next time. It could be me.' He grinned. 'Or maybe I'll beat him. Maybe I'll kill all his rooks and take all his power and bring back my dad from the dead.'

Ash stared at him. Perhaps Mark really was crazy and believed all this stuff he was coming out with. Sheep skulls, the old ways, human sacrifice, killing rooks, this creepy Bone Jack character. Bringing back his dad from the dead.

But another, darker thought played through his mind – that Mark wasn't mad at all. Ash had seen weird, impossible things with his own eyes – the unearthly stag boy fleeing the hounds, the shadows that had chased him along the path, the black feather oozing evil. Maybe it was the world that had gone mad, not Mark.

He shivered.

Mark laughed and jabbed at the fire with a stick. 'Don't look so worried. You probably saw a poacher, that's all. We're not the only ones out and about in the woods at night.'

Ash forced a smile. 'Yeah, well, this place is freaky. All those sheep skulls in the trees. Did you do that?'

'Yeah.'

'There must be at least a dozen of them,' said Ash. 'Where did you get them from?'

'They were our sheep,' said Mark. 'Some of the ones that were slaughtered in the foot-and-mouth outbreak.'

'They burned the carcasses and buried them. I was there. I saw it. You dug them up again and stuck their skulls in trees? What for?'

Mark shrugged, looked away.

Ash changed the subject. 'There was something weird going on up near Stag's Leap the other day,' he said. 'Hounds chasing a stag boy.'

'The Stag Chase isn't for another couple of weeks yet.'

'Twelve days. I know. That's what's so weird. I saw the whole thing. They ran right past me. Then they vanished into thin air.'

'Yeah?' Suddenly Mark seemed guarded, unreadable.

'Yeah. Callie was out there too, but she said she didn't see them. She said you'd know something about it.'

Mark smiled. 'You saw the ghosts.'

'Right,' said Ash. 'Ghosts.'

'You don't believe in them. I get that. I didn't used to believe in them either. But there are plenty of ghosts out in the mountains. You'll see. This land's all blood and bone. All the lost and the dead out there.'

'Ghosts and blood and human sacrifice. It's crazy. You should just listen to yourself.'

Mark looked sideways at him. 'It's like I told you. The land's dying. Shadows in a wasteland, that's what we are, Ash Tyler. So the old ways are back and things have to be put right.'

'You're not making any sense,' said Ash. 'All this dark stuff. It's all just old legends and ghost stories. You're not supposed to believe stories like that.'

'Bone Jack.' Mark hunched up, rocked himself. 'Bone Jack took my dad's life.'

'Your dad took his own life.'

Mark didn't answer. He rocked and rocked. Then he stopped, straightened. 'Those boys you saw,' he said, 'the stag boy and the hounds – they were ghosts.'

The pounding of their feet on the parched ground. The stag boy's stumbling run, the exhaustion on his face. 'They weren't ghosts,' Ash said, uneasy. 'They looked unreal, but that was just the heat haze. It makes everything look like a mirage. They were flesh and blood, like us.'

'Flesh-and-blood people don't vanish into thin air.'

'What about the boys who were here earlier? The ones who were dancing around the fire? Were they real boys or ghosts?'

'You weren't a hound boy last year, were you?'

'No. I wasn't old enough. You have to be fifteen.'

'If you'd been a hound, you'd know. There's all sorts of rituals and stuff if you're a hound.'

'Yeah, I've heard about that, the hounds hassling the stag boy, playing pranks, that sort of thing.'

Mark poked the fire with the stick again. The flames guttered and leaped.

'In the old days,' he said, 'it was serious. The hounds distanced themselves from the stag boy, because if they caught him in the Stag Chase, they had to kill him. It meant he was weak, see. Too weak to outrun them. And if he was weak then that meant the land was weak and blight would follow. The crops would fail. The animals would ail and die. There'd be sickness, hunger. Then people would die. So if the hounds caught the stag boy, they killed him. A blood offering to the land, to make it strong again. A sacrifice. That's bad, isn't it? That's savage. But sometimes you have to do bad things to make things right. Sometimes you don't have a choice.'

The strange stag boy running, desperate, frightened. Running for his life. That final awful scream.

A blood offering.

'A sacrifice to what? Bone Jack?'

Mark shrugged. 'To the land. It's a bargain with the gods of the land, I suppose. People have been sacrificing animals and humans to gods for thousands of years, all over the world.'

'Yeah, well, so what? Everyone knows those sorts of things used to happen a long time ago. Torture and witch burnings and human sacrifice and other stuff.'

'Yeah,' said Mark. 'This is the twenty-first century. We're civilised now. We don't sacrifice people these days. When the land is sick, the government sends men in biohazard suits to kill and quarantine everything. The Stag Chase is just a glorified cross-country race, with costumes and stupid masks and hotdog vans and charity fundraising and TV crews and tourists. But sometimes, when things get really bad, it gets like ancient times again. It's all blood and darkness again. That's why you mustn't be the stag boy.'

'You really think the hounds are going to kill me?'

'Not the hounds. Me.'

'You? You're full of it, Mark.'

'Life for life,' said Mark. 'The stag boy's life in exchange for my dad's. I'm going to bring my dad back, make things right. It's the stag boy who has to die, not you personally. I don't want to kill you. That's why you have to pull out of the race. Let some other boy be the stag.'

'This is mad,' said Ash. He watched Mark in the fire's

glow. 'Really mad. You're not going to kill me. You're not going to kill anyone. Come down off the mountain with me. We'll talk to my mum. Maybe you can stay with us for a while, get yourself sorted.'

'I am sorted. I'm where I need to be. It's not like when we were kids, Ash. I'm not going to come home with you and have some supper and then tomorrow we go off downhilling on our bikes somewhere. Those days are gone.'

'Callie's worried sick about you. Don't you even care?'

'Callie's just a kid.'

'She not a kid. She's fourteen and you're all she's got left.'

'She's OK. She can look after herself. Besides, he was her dad too. I'm doing all this for her as much as for me. We need our dad back. Both of us.'

Suddenly Ash felt very tired. 'It's late,' he said. 'I'm going to head off home.'

'Running away again, Ash Tyler?'

'If you say so. I don't need any more of this crap. Bad enough with Dad at home.'

'At least you've still got a dad.'

'Yeah, I know.'

'Go on then. Don't let me stop you.'

'I'll come back. Soon.'

'Whatever. I'll either be here or I won't.'

'Do you need anything? Food or blankets or some-thing?' Ash stood up. His jaw throbbed where Mark had hit him. He felt light-headed, delirious.

As if from a long way off he heard Mark say, 'Thanks, but I've got everything I need.'

Mark stretched out on the ground next to the fire. Closed his eyes.

Ash walked away. In his mind he heard Mark's voice again, saying, 'I don't want to kill you ... let some other boy be the stag.' It would be easy, so easy to let it go, to walk away from the Stag Chase and whatever madness Mark was spinning around it. Let some other boy be the stag. Let everything be that other boy's problem.

But he couldn't do that, wouldn't do that. He wasn't about to throw away months of training just because a few strange things had happened and Mark was making wild threats.

He walked on, into a darkness that stretched from horizon to horizon. A night dusted with stars, crowded with ghosts.

NINE

The light was on in the hallway when he got home. He crept upstairs. Darkness under the door of the spare room, where Dad was sleeping. A crack of yellowy light under Mum's door. He knocked softly and went in.

She was sitting up in bed, reading a book. She looked tired and sad, eyes puffy as if she'd been crying. But she smiled and patted the edge of the bed so he sat there.

'So did you find Mark?'

'Yeah.'

'How did it go? Was it OK?'

'I suppose. I don't know. It was weird. He said a lot of mad stuff. He's mucking around out there, eating road kill and shooting rooks and rabbits and living off the land and stuff.'

'Eating road kill?' She pulled a face. 'And rooks? Yuck. So he's camping out, is he?'

'Yeah.'

'Maybe that's what he needs to do right now. It'll pass. When autumn comes and it's raining and cold, he'll soon go back to his grandpa's house.'

'Yeah, I suppose. How's Dad been?'

'Sleeping. That's all he seems to have done since he got home. I took him up some soup earlier. He hadn't touched his lunch.'

'What's wrong with him, Mum? Why did he go off drinking for two days instead of coming straight home like he usually does? He looks ill, really ill. And now he's shutting himself up in that room and acting crazy.'

'He's been through a lot. He just needs to get his bearings and settle back into civilian life. It's hard but he'll be OK.'

'Callie thinks he's got shell shock.'

'She's a smart girl. It's crossed my mind too.'

'Right. So shouldn't we do something? Call a doctor or something?'

'It's not that simple,' she said. 'There's already an army counsellor waiting to see him, but he won't go and he won't have the counsellor come to the house either. He's not ready yet, I suppose.'

'When will he be ready?'

'I don't know. Anyway, he's only been back a couple of days. Maybe once he's adjusted to being home again, he'll be all right.'

'What if he isn't? What if Callie's right and he's got shell shock?'

'We call it post-traumatic stress disorder these days.'

'Post-traumatic stress then. What if he's got that?'

'Then we'll deal with it.'

'What if we can't?'

'We will.'

'Yeah, but what if we can't? What's the back-up plan? What if we're not enough?'

'It might take some time but we'll get through this,' she said. 'He's still your dad, the same dad who taught you how to ride a bike and pitch a tent and abseil down a mountain. Don't forget that. He's just a bit lost right now.'

'Suppose he stays lost for ever? He might...' He couldn't say it. 'You know, like Mark's dad.'

'He won't,' she said sharply. So sharply that he knew she'd had the same thought. Then she changed the subject. 'Not long now until the Stag Chase.'

'Yeah, twelve more days.'

'Are you ready for it?'

'I think so. I hope so, anyway.'

'You'll be careful, won't you?' she said. Anxiety creeping into her voice. She'd never liked him running in the mountains. Anything could happen to you, all alone out there, she'd say.

But she'd never stopped him.

'Training is one thing,' she said. 'You can decide your own route and set your own pace when you're training. The Stag Chase is different. It's a race, a tough race. The pressure will be on. Don't let it get to you. Don't do anything dangerous just to win it.'

'I won't, Mum.'

'Promise?'

'I promise.'

'OK then.' She smiled. 'You look like you could do with some sleep.'

'Yeah, it's been a long day.'

'Bed then.'

In his room, he lay in his bed as if it was a boat in the silent ocean of the night. Tiredness washed through him, and he surrendered to it.

TEN

The days passed, glassy with heat, the nights as thick as tar. Dad shut in his room and Mum restless, spending most of her time in the garden or visiting friends. It seemed to Ash that life was on hold, all of them adrift on a windless sea, choosing not to look at the storm clouds gathering on the horizon. He slept, he ran, he ate, he played computer games, read books, tried to stay focused.

Every day now, he saw other boys out running in the mountains. They ran in pairs and sometimes in packs. Hound boys, training for the race. Some were boys he'd never seen before, from towns and villages further out in the mountains. Others he knew from school, boys he'd been friendly with until he'd beaten them in the trials and become the stag boy. Sometimes they passed him, silent, their eyes cold and hostile. Sometimes they ran alongside him for a while, jostled him, veered off laughing. He hated it but he knew the score. The stag boy was always an outcast in the weeks between winning the trials and running in the Stag Chase itself. So Ash kept his gaze on the path ahead, kept running. It was him against them now until after the race.

Twice he saw a distant figure silhouetted against the sky and he was sure it was Mark. Standing above and apart from it all, watching. He remembered Mark's words again and shivered. *It's the stag boy who has to die . . . I don't want to kill you.*

After a week of being hassled by hound boys, Ash started to run a different route – one that took him far away from where the other boys ran, far from the Cullen farm and Stag's Leap. He took the little paths, the ancient paths, and ran north then northwest, beyond the wide farming valleys and into the wildlands.

He almost tripped over the dog.

It was lying in a hollow where the path tucked down between high banks of gorse. A big dog, with a rough black and grey coat matted with muck and dried blood.

Someone's pet, lost or dumped out here in the mountains, in the middle of nowhere.

Ash crouched beside it. It didn't move, didn't even seem to be breathing. It looked dead but, in case it wasn't, he spoke reassuringly to it. 'All right,' he said. 'It's all right, boy. I won't hurt you.'

No reaction. The dog lay there looking like a moth-eaten fur coat that had been dragged through the dirt.

It must have owners somewhere, people who cared about it, missed it. They were probably out searching for it this very moment, worried sick. He pushed his fingers into the thick hair around its neck. He felt for a collar but there wasn't one.

Maybe it was a stray after all, living wild out here, far away from people.

He ran his hands along its body, felt its bones sharp through its heavy coat. Every rib, every vertebra.

A low rumble in its throat. Ash snatched away his hand.

Its eyes half opened: light amber eyes, wolf eyes. A gaze as ancient and wild as the mountains themselves.

Ash drew a sharp breath. 'Where did you come from then?' he said softly. 'How did you end up out here?'

The wolf-dog curled its lip as if it wanted to snarl and snap but didn't have the strength.

The spell broke. It was just a dog after all, Ash thought, a half-starved feral stray.

Feral or not, he couldn't leave it to die. He rocked

back on his heels and thought about what to do. The dog was too big and heavy to carry back through the mountains. He needed help. He stood up, looked all around, listened. They were a long way from the main trails, but sometimes hikers left the beaten track and ventured out here along the little twisting paths.

Not this morning though.

Something moved on the mountainside. A clot of darkness, racing towards them. He squinted into the sun, trying to see what was casting the shadow, but there was only the empty land and the empty sky. The shadow sped closer, coming straight for him. He ducked as it reached him. Then it stopped. It lay over and all around him. He looked up from within its darkness, his heart thudding. Nothing there but the scrub of gorse and bracken, the distant peaks.

Nothing that could cast a shadow like this.

The wolf-dog growled softly, a warning.

The shadow shook apart, shattering into fragments that morphed into inky, ethereal human figures that fled this way and that.

Then the shadow-figures thinned, dissolved into sunlight until there was nothing there any more.

Ash stood up, heart thumping. He scanned the horizon in every direction.

No shadows. No people around who might have cast them.

Yet he could still sense their presence. Not evil exactly but savage and predatory, lurking out of sight somewhere on the raw rocky land. And him and the wolf-dog out here alone, miles from anywhere, fragile specks of bone and blood and soft flesh.

He felt like a mouse waiting for a hawk to strike.

But nothing struck. The shadow figures were gone.

If they had ever been there at all.

He switched his attention back to the wolf-dog. He took a bottle from his backpack and dribbled water into its mouth. It licked its lips and swallowed. He carried on feeding it water until the bottle was empty. By then, the dog's gaze had lost some of its hardness.

It still didn't look exactly friendly though.

And it needed a lot more than water. It needed serious help, a vet. Maybe it was already too far gone even for that.

He knew his mobile wouldn't work out here. He could never get a signal in the mountains beyond Tolley Carn. It was like a black hole for mobile phones. He only brought the thing out with him because Mum insisted. He tried it anyway, just in case. Sure enough, a blue No Signal message flashed up on the screen.

He could run back to the village, fetch Dad. But he was miles out. It would take too long to get home and back again and he couldn't rely on Dad for help anyway, not any more.

It was all down to him.

His best bet was to reach a road and flag down a car.

'I'm going to fetch help,' he told the dog. 'I'll be back soon.' He rolled his eyes at himself. Explaining to a dog. Idiot.

He climbed up onto the higher ground above the path. A couple of hundred metres away, a rocky outcrop as tall as a house jutted from the mountainside. He scrambled up it and stood at its summit. From here he could see for miles. But there was no one in sight, no roads, no buildings, nothing. As if civilisation no longer existed.

Ahead of him, the mountainside dipped down into a wide, deep valley with a straggly thicket of thorn trees running most of its length.

A tiny movement about the trees, a breath of bluish smoke unwinding.

Campers, most likely.

They'd do.

He returned to the path and ran down it until a hunch of mountain hid the thorn trees and the path zagged in the wrong direction. He left it behind and loped across rough terrain, through bracken and gorse, over rocks and humps of gnarly root. Then he was out of the rough, running easily across a greasy stretch of short wiry grass. He splashed across a shallow, sluggish stream that had once been a small river and barged his way through the spiky wall of thorn trees onto open ground.

Ahead stood an ancient shepherds' bothy, a small rectangular building with thick stone walls, a turf roof, two deep-set windows hazed with grime. Smoke drifted from a little crooked chimney.

There was a doorway, but in place of a door hung a curtain of strings of bird skulls and small bones. The breeze clattered them against each other like Halloween wind chimes.

Behind the bone-strings, the interior of the bothy was a deep quiet darkness.

A flurry of movement in the trees behind him, harsh cries, beating air.

He turned. Rooks, scores of them. They dropped down onto branches, stretched their necks at him. They rattled their night-black feathers, gun-metal beaks wide open, screaming at him with their rough voices.

The dread he'd felt on the mountain when the shadow dropped over him rushed back. He shot a quick glance at the bothy and glimpsed a face through the window, blurry and dim as a fish moving through murky water. Then it was gone again.

Ash raced back through the trees the way he had come.

And a man stepped out in front of him.

ELEVEN

Ash hurled himself between the trees. Thorns ripped at his clothes, hair, skin. He crashed through twigs and bright green leaves and raced towards the open ground beyond. Then his foot hooked on a loop of bramble and threw him forward. He twisted as he fell and crashed sideways into a tree.

Heavy hands seized his shoulders and wrenched him round. He glimpsed a raggedy coat, a floppy wide-brimmed hat, grey stubble, mad blue eyes. The man looked vaguely familiar, in the way that a stranger who'd asked you for directions a week ago might look familiar. But there was no time to think about that now. Ash bucked his body. He threw out a wild kick and felt his foot connect with bone. His fist sank into the thickness of the man's coat.

The man didn't let go. Instead his fingers dug deeper

into Ash's shoulders.

'What are you doing here, boy?' he said. His breath smelled like dead leaves. 'What are you after, eh?'

'Nothing.' Ash's voice came out in a pathetic whisper.

'Liar.'

'I came to get help, that's all. I found a dog.'

'What dog? I don't see a dog. Where is it?'

'Not here. It's further up the mountain. It's sick, just lying on the ground like it can't get up.'

The man's grip loosened a little bit. 'What sort of dog? What's it look like?'

'I don't know what sort. A big dog, black and grey and covered in muck. It's got eyes like a wolf's and it's really thin. I could feel all its bones. I thought it was dead at first but it wasn't. I think it's dying though.'

'Eyes like a wolf's, eh?' The man's hands slid away from Ash's shoulders. Instantly, Ash launched himself along the path.

Something shot past him, a bolt of untidy black like a bird flying parallel to the ground.

The man was in front of him again.

Ash froze, his breath coming in quick panicky gasps. It was impossible. There was no way the man could have got in front of him so quickly.

No way.

Ash tried to speak but the words wouldn't come out.

'Don't try running off again,' said the man. There was no menace in his voice. There didn't need to be. 'Take me to this dog with eyes like a wolf's. Quick, now.'

Ash sucked in air.

There was no choice except to do what the man told him. In silence, Ash led him across the stream to the rough ground beyond. He was shaking so badly his legs barely obeyed him. Get a grip, he told himself. Breathe. Focus. Talk to him. Get him to like you a bit so maybe he won't kill you.

He forced out the words. 'Is that where you live, in that old bothy?'

'Aye.'

'I've run out here a few times but I've never seen it before.'

The man grunted. 'There are lots of things folks don't see.'

He walked with a long, unhurried stride, the way Ash had seen shepherds walk. Maybe that was all the man really was, a shepherd, still living out in the mountains even though the sheep were long gone.

'My name's Ash,' he said. He felt ridiculous, struggling to make small talk with his captor. 'I'm from Thornditch. I just came out for a run and then I found the dog and came looking for help. I didn't mean to disturb you or to trespass or anything.'

'I know who you are,' said the man.

Fear flooded through Ash again. He fell silent.

They reached the path and slogged uphill. The morning sun was hot on Ash's back. Tiny brown birds flitted and chattered in the gorse. A shiny dung beetle blundered across the path.

It all seemed so ordinary.

Except that he was walking with a freak who was wearing a thick coat and a hat on a hot day and who moved with supernatural speed. The man could be a serial killer for all Ash knew, and they were miles from anywhere, miles from help. He could be murdered and buried out here and his body would never be found. No one would ever know.

Sweat crawled down his spine.

The dog was exactly as he'd left it only now its eyes were closed again. Ash stared down at it. 'It looks dead,' he said. 'We're too late. It's dead.'

The man grunted. 'Dead or not, back he'll go.'

'Back where?'

'Back to the valley, with me.'

'Where your bothy is?'

'Aye. Back there, back where he belongs.'

'So he's your dog?'

The man shook his head. 'Ain't a dog. That's a wolf.'

Ash's eyes widened. 'A wolf? Did he escape from a zoo or something?'

'He's a wild wolf.'

'He can't be. There aren't any wild wolves in Britain. Not any more. Not for hundreds of years.'

'I know that. That's why he has to come back with me.'

The man hunkered down next to the wolf-dog. It didn't move.

Dead, thought Ash. Dead, dead. They were too late.

The man whispered something, singsong words too softly spoken for Ash to catch. The wolf-dog's ears twitched and its eyes flickered open again. The man smiled. He slid his hands along its body then under it and hefted the beast up into his arms.

Ash could have run then. Unnaturally fast though the man was, Ash would surely be able to outrun him now he had the wolf-dog in his arms.

But he didn't run. He wasn't afraid any more. The man was more interested in the wolf-dog than in him.

'Will he be OK?' said Ash.

'Mebbe.'

'He looks in a bad way. We should get him to a vet.'

'No vets up here. Just me.' said the man. His eyes narrowed, slits of blue. 'He shouldn't be here. Something brought him through, brought him from long ago. You know owt about that?'

Ash shook his head. 'I just found him here.'

'You know owt about that lad that's been killing rooks?'

The three dead rooks hanging from a tree at Mark's camp.

Again, Ash shook his head. 'I haven't seen anyone killing rooks.'

Not quite a lie.

'Aye, well,' said the man. 'Best go home now, lad.'

Now Ash remembered where he'd seen him before. The face in the dark, turning away. 'You were in the woods the other night,' he said. 'I saw you.'

The man grunted, said nothing.

'Bone Jack,' said Ash. 'That's what Mark called you.'

Something flickered in the man's eyes. Then it was gone again.

'You ain't my business today,' the man said. 'Go home.'

He turned his back on Ash and headed back down the path, walking with the same easy stride as before despite the weight of the wolf-dog in his arms.

Ash watched him go until he was out of sight.

Then the spell that had held him broke. He ran all the way home.

When he got there, Dad was screaming.

TWELVE

The screams came from the living room. Shattered glass glittered on the dark green carpet. Broken mirror on the wall above it. A fallen vase spilling flowers and water. The sofa upturned.

The room stank of whisky.

Ash stood rooted to the spot.

The TV was running the news, the volume turned up loud. Flyblown children stranded on a tiny island of mud in a swirling tide of brown floodwater. The shadow of a helicopter passing over them. A bomb in a marketplace, dozens dead or injured. A dazed woman walking through the carnage. Apples spilled everywhere.

So strange. All those apples among rubble and twisted metal and blood and bodies.

A yelping scream from somewhere in the room, like the cry of a seagull. And another yelp, and another.

Blood on the carpet, on the coffee table, dark and glossy.

Ash's stomach clenched.

Dad, sitting on the floor next to the sofa, knees drawn up to his chest, one side of his face pressed against the wall. Staring into space, his eyes wide and crazy with terror.

Ash followed the direction of Dad's gaze.

He was staring at a black feather on the floor. A feather like the one Ash had found in his bedroom. Exactly like it.

And no sign of Mum.

Blood on the carpet, and Mum nowhere in sight.

Ash's head was full of noise: the TV, Dad, the ocean roar of his own blood rushing through his veins. The feather on the floor, shadow pulsing out of it.

How did it get there?

It couldn't be the same feather he'd dropped in the river. So where had it come from? Why was it in the room with Dad?

Ash forced himself to look away. 'Where's Mum? Dad! What have you done?' he said. He couldn't catch his breath. The words juddered out, drowning in the racket from the TV.

Yelp.

'Dad!'

Yelp.

The TV spewing noise. Ash hunted for the remote control. Nowhere to be found. He wrenched the TV's plug out of the socket instead. The screen popped and went black.

Dad stopped yelping.

'Dad!'

Slowly Dad turned to look at him. Red-rimmed eyes. He looked exhausted, like he hadn't slept for weeks.

Ash was shaking, his whole body trembling. 'Dad, where's Mum?'

'She's not here.' Mumbling, slurring his words.

'Where is she?'

Dad curled up tighter, pressed his forehead to his knees, rocked himself back and forth. Useless.

'Did you hurt her?' said Ash. 'Where is she? You'd better not have hurt her.'

Nothing.

Ash raced into the hallway, yelling for Mum.

Then he heard her voice.

She was upstairs on the landing, leaning out over the banister. He took the stairs two at a time.

She was all right. He could see that. There wasn't a mark on her. But he needed her to tell him so he asked anyway.

'I'm OK,' she said. 'Calm down. I'm fine.'

'There's blood,' he said. Still breathless, trembling. 'There's blood on the living-room floor.'

She ushered him into her bedroom and closed the door. 'Your dad cut his hand, that's all,' she said. 'It's his blood, not mine.'

'How? What happened?'

'I didn't see, but I think he punched the mirror. His hand was still bleeding heavily when I got there but it's not that bad really. The cuts aren't deep. I've put a dressing on it and I don't think it needs stitches.'

'I thought he'd hurt you.'

'Oh, Ash. He'd never hurt me. Or you. He'd rather die than hurt either of us.'

Ash nodded but he didn't believe her. Dad wasn't himself, wasn't rational. Right now, he seemed capable of anything.

'What happened, Mum?' His hands were still shaking. He tried to steady them but he couldn't. 'Why did he flip out like that?'

'I don't know,' she said. 'I went out for a couple of hours. When I got back, the living room was a mess and he was sitting in the middle of it with the TV on full blast and an empty whisky bottle next to him. I couldn't find the remote control to turn off the TV.'

'I pulled the plug out.'

'Good. I didn't think of that. I was panicking, I suppose. Anyway, he was bleeding so I ran and got a dressing and bandaged his hand. Then I came up here to phone the doctor.'

'Right,' said Ash. 'Is he coming?'

'Yes, of course. He'll be here as soon as he can.'

Footsteps on the stairs and then the landing, slow and heavy. Ash froze. The door to Dad's room slammed shut.

Mum sighed. 'Back in his bolthole again. I'd better go down and clear up the living room before the doctor gets here. Will you give me a hand?'

Ash didn't want to. He was still trembling. He wanted to retreat into his room, like Dad, and play computer games and loud music until his brain fried.

But that would have to wait.

They crept passed the door to Dad's room and went downstairs. They fetched the vacuum cleaner, a dustpan and brush, a couple of cloths from the cupboard under the stairs. Then they went into the living room.

Ash's gaze went straight to the black feather. But the feather was gone. He looked around for it on the floor. Nothing.

Where the hell was it?

He searched again. No sign of it.

No one had been in here except Dad. Dad, who'd been staring at the feather, terror written on his face.

Ash's thoughts raced. Another black feather in the house was more than just a coincidence. It was a message, a warning with some sort of supernatural force. And Dad had understood that too, felt its power. But how had the second feather got into the house? Someone must have brought it and left it in the room with Dad.

Someone else had been here. Who?

His mind was spinning. Dad must know, must have seen someone, but he couldn't ask him, not right now.

Who'd been here? Who would do this?

None of it made sense.

'Come on, Ash,' said Mum. 'Snap out of it. I thought you were supposed to be helping.'

'Yeah,' said Ash. 'I am going to help. Sorry.'

He picked up the vase and mopped up the spilled water soaking the carpet. Then he looked up.

There was blood on the window, a smeary handprint where Dad must have pressed against it after he'd punched the mirror. Ash wiped a cloth over it, but the blood wouldn't come off. He stared at it, puzzled, still too much in a daze about Dad and the black feather to think straight.

Then it hit him.

The bloody print was on the outside of the window.

Someone had stood out there, watching Dad. Someone with blood on his hands.

He looked past the handprint, across the lawn to the line of trees beyond. Something stared sightlessly back at him. A sheep skull, wedged in the fork of a branch.

Mark, he thought. The black feather, the bloody handprint, the skull. All this was Mark's work. Had to be.

Mum was picking up pieces of the broken mirror. 'I need another cloth,' said Ash. 'Back in a minute.' He stumbled past her with the wet cloth still in his hand. Out into the hallway, out through the front door into sunlight. He stood outside the living-room window, wiped away the blood on the glass while Mum still crouched indoors, with her back to him. Then he yanked the skull from the tree and shoved it deep under the hedge.

He closed his eyes, raised his face to the sun. Let sunlight sear through his eyelids, blinding white blankness.

After a few seconds, he opened his eyes. Blinked away the sun glare.

Mark had been here, freaking out Dad, playing mind games.

Why? A warning, perhaps. A threat. Mark had told him not to run in the Stag Chase and Ash had refused to pull out. Now this.

'Go to hell, Mark Cullen,' said Ash, under his breath. 'Leave my family alone and go to hell.'

THIRTEEN

The doctor came, spent five minutes with Dad, five with Mum, left a small brown bottle of pills on the kitchen table. 'Call me if things don't improve,' he said. Cheery voice, a smile and wave, then his car grinding down the gravel drive and away.

Ash stayed in his room all afternoon, all evening. Mum knocked but he didn't respond and she didn't come in. 'I've left some supper for you on the landing,' she said.

He waited until he heard her go downstairs before he opened the door. A plate piled with sandwiches. He wanted to leave them there, some sort of protest against...what? Dad. Mum. Everything. But hunger got the better of him.

While he was eating, he tried to remember exactly what Mark had said to him in the woods that night. About the Stag Chase, Bone Jack, the old ways.

He went online and searched for 'Bone Jack'. There were only a handful of hits. The first link led to a page on a medical-school website, dedicated to an anatomical skeleton the students had nicknamed Bone Jack.

A second link took him to a page on an online encyclopedia of folklore and legends.

> *Bone Jack: an ancient and obscure folkloric figure, particular to the mountainous region around Coldbrook in northern England. Some folklorists place Bone Jack in a loose category of mythic figures associated with nature, wildness and renewal – a category that also includes the Green Man, Lailoken, Myrddin Wyllt, Taliesin and many others. The few early writings that refer to the Bone Jack figure further associate him with the cycle of life and death and with guardianship of the boundary between this world and the Otherworld, attributing him with the ability to shapeshift between human and bird forms – a characteristic that further relates to the pre-Christian Celtic belief that the souls of the dead assume bird form to make their journey to Annwn, the Celtic Otherworld.*

Ash sighed. As ever on the internet, every answer only seemed to lead to more questions. Only the name Taliesin was familiar, something or other they'd done in school, though of course he hadn't paid enough attention and now he couldn't remember what it was. Nothing for it but to follow the links and read.

He read about Taliesin, a sixth-century Welsh bard whose name meant 'shining brow' and whose story was part history and part myth – servant to a sorceress called Ceridwen, a shapeshifter, a poet nowadays best remembered for his most famous poem, *The Battle of the Trees*. Ash clicked on another link and read about Lailoken, also from the sixth century, a mad prophet, a wild man who lived deep in the Caledonian Forest and had an affinity with wild creatures. And Myrddin Wyllt, another crazy wild man of the forest, a character some people thought was the original Merlin.

Last, he looked up the Green Man, and he was the strangest and most ancient figure of them all, leaves and shoots growing from his flesh, a spirit of springtime, rebirth and growth.

Bone Jack had things in common with all of them. He was a wild man who lived in a wild place and seemed to prefer the company of birds and beasts to that of humans. A shapeshifter, a shaman moving across different realities. The Green Man's dark alter ego in nature's great cycle of life and death and renewal.

It seemed impossible that the wild man he'd met in the mountains could really be Bone Jack, a mythic figure, some sort of dark fairy tale from a distant past. Ash remembered the unnatural speed the man had seemed to move at, but there could be a rational explanation for that, couldn't there? There could have been two men out there, brothers, almost identical in their tramp clothing. One behind him on the path and one ahead, lying in wait. And maybe Ash had fled from one brother only to run straight into the second.

But much as Ash wanted to believe in his rational explanation, it somehow seemed less likely than the possibility that the man really was Bone Jack – wild, ancient, a myth come to life – and that there really were ghosts in the mountains, spectral hound boys racing across the land. And then there was Mark, caught up in it all, spinning out of control, threatening Ash, chasing some insane scheme to bring back his father from the Otherworld.

The Otherworld, Annwn. If Bone Jack really was the guardian of the boundary between life and death then that meant Mark would have to somehow get past Bone Jack to reach his father. He remembered what Mark had said that night in the woods, about killing Bone Jack's rooks and taking his power.

And if Mark was attacking Bone Jack then maybe he would come after Mark, after all of them. Maybe it was Bone Jack who sent out the spectral hound boys to hunt, to kill.

He shook his head, laughed at himself. The whole thing was like something from a book or a movie, not something from real life.

He shut down the laptop and went to the window to close the curtains. Taped to the window pane was a scrap of paper with something scrawled on it. Frowning, he pulled it off.

'We need to talk,' it said. 'My camp, tomorrow. Or I'll find you.'

Mark. He must have sneaked up here to Ash's room when he'd come to play mind games with Dad.

'Get lost, Mark,' said Ash, under his breath. He crumpled the paper into a tiny ball and tossed it into the wastepaper basket.

He switched off the light and lay on his back in the dark. He listened. The night was full of little sounds, the tap of twigs against the window, leaves stirring in the breeze, the distant fluting of an owl. Every sound made Ash's heart race. Now he thought he heard footsteps on the gravel, coming up the drive. Someone prowling out-side. The feather that had been in the living room, still somewhere in the house, oozing evil. Summoning dark forces like a curse.

Anything might be out there, coming for him through the clammy night.

Another tiny sound, inside the house this time. Then another, and another. He lay still, breathing quietly, con-centrating. The sounds consolidated into actions: a door opening and closing softly, the pad of bare feet along the landing, down the stairs.

Dad, wandering around the house in the dark.

There was a long silence. Then the click of the front door shutting.

Ash rolled out of bed and went to the window. The waxing moon hung above Tolley Carn like a bent silver coin.

A shadow slipped through the darkness that edged the drive. Then it moved out into the wash of moonlight at the gate.

Dad.

Ash watched him go out through the gate, turn right along the lane, vanish into the night. Nothing up the lane except mountains and a few farms.

No one Dad would visit at this time of night.

Panic raced through Ash. Dad out in the mountains, disturbed and alone. Anything could happen to him.

He switched on the bedside lamp, pulled on his clothes. Briefly he thought about waking Mum. Then he dismissed the idea; she was worried enough already, no point making things worse. So he crept through the house, out of the front door, loped down the drive. No sign of Dad on the lane, but Ash knew which way he'd gone.

He started to run.

The hot dark prickled against his skin. He ran under a skyful of stars. The moon above the jagged skyline. Silence. Nothing moving in the hedges or fields, no breeze rustling the leaves, not even the distant drone of a car. Only the thump of his feet, his heartbeat, the rhythm of his breath.

He slowed around the bend. Dad couldn't be far ahead. Ash didn't want to come charging out of the night, scare him.

The lane stretched away, silvery grey in the moonlight.

No sign of Dad.

Tall hedges on either side, dry-stone wall further along the lane. No turnings. Nowhere to go except straight ahead.

But Dad wasn't there.

Then Ash remembered that there was a little stile somewhere here, hidden away in the thick cover of dusty leaves. Dad must have gone that way. There was nowhere else.

He found the crease in the hedge where the stile was, pushed through dense foliage, felt a lash of tingling heat across the back of his hand where it brushed against a nettle.

Beyond the stile, a faint footpath slanted across a scrubby field and on the far side strode a shadowy figure, quick and purposeful.

Ash followed.

Through the mountains, black and soft grey like a charcoal sketch, intense here and smudged there. A burned world. The air thick and warm with a nip to it. Moths grazing his skin.

Silence except for his own footfalls. The shrill scolding of a bird nearby, disturbed by his presence. A thin shriek, some tiny mammal taken by owl or stoat or fox.

Sometimes he saw Dad in the distance. Sometimes he lost sight of him and panicked and hurried and had to stop himself from calling out.

They were up on Stag's Leap now, rock veined with moonlight, and Dad was standing at the edge, the very edge.

Ash stood rooted to the spot, watching, his heart racing.

But Dad didn't jump. He pulled something out of his pocket, held it out over the drop, let go of it. A little dart of shadow spiralling down.

The black feather.

It had to be.

Then Dad turned, came back down the slope to the path. Ash waited, then followed again, along a narrow track that hugged the shoulder of the mountain.

Ahead lay the Cullen farm, dark and silent. Dad stopped at the gate, stood there for a while. Then he turned, looked straight towards Ash. Must have known he was there all along. Ash walked along the track towards him.

'Home now then, lad?' said Dad. Soft-voiced, gentle.

'Yeah.'

They walked on for a while.

'You dropped something over the edge,' said Ash. 'I saw you, up on the Leap. What was it?'

Dad didn't answer.

'Why did you come out here, Dad?'

Dad drew a long breath, let it out slowly. 'Tom Cullen,' he said. 'He was my best mate when we were boys. Like you and Mark we were. We used to go off hunting, fishing, climbing. Not so much later on though. Him with the farm, me with the army. Marriage, kids, all that. Time passes. And now he's dead.'

'It's not your fault.'

'Isn't it? I could have been a better friend to him. I could have kept in touch, spent time with him when I was home on leave. I meant to. I just never got round to it and now it's too late.'

'You weren't to know.'

'That's the thing though. I should have known. Him out there on his own after Ella died, two kids to raise and a farm to run. Then there was the foot-and-mouth outbreak, his stock slaughtered. I suppose he'd just used up all his strength by then. No reserves left. I should have been here. I should have done something.'

'You were overseas,' said Ash. 'You were fighting a war.'

'People keep dying around me,' said Dad. 'And I keep surviving.'

'Is that what happened in the war?'

'It's what war is. People killing each other. People dying. You try not to be one of them. If you're lucky, you get to come home in one piece.'

'It was really bad, wasn't it?'

'Yeah, it was really bad.'

They walked on in silence for a while.

'That thing you dropped from the Leap,' said Ash. 'I know what it was.'

'You do?'

'Yeah, I do. It was the black feather that was on the floor in the living room.'

'Yeah.' Sharp and hard. 'How did you know?'

Ash shrugged. 'Just a guess. You were staring at it, then it disappeared with you when you left the room. Where did it come from?'

'A bird, I suppose.'

'Ha-ha. At least you're still making rubbish jokes anyway.'

'All I'm good for these days.'

'That feather though,' said Ash. 'Tell me about that.'

'It reminded me of something from a long time ago. Stupid, really.'

'Tell me, Dad.'

Dad shrugged, sighed, shut down.

'How did it get in the house?' said Ash. Pushing, not letting Dad retreat into another of his silences. 'Who brought it in?'

'I don't know,' said Dad. 'There was someone else there. I saw him but I don't know who he was. A face like a skull at the window. Hands dripping with blood.'

He stopped, ran his fingers through his hair. 'I thought it was...someone or something that came back with me from the desert, something vengeful. Haunting me. I see them sometimes, in my dreams. The dead. Then there was that feather and...maybe I'm just...'

Breaking up, falling apart again.

'Just what?'

'I don't know. Hallucinating or something.'

'You're not,' said Ash. 'It wasn't anything to do with the war. It's something else, something to do with the Stag Chase.'

'I saw a feather like that once before,' said Dad. 'Years ago, long before you were born, I trained for the Stag Chase out here. And one day a bird flew into me, a crow or a rook or something. I don't know why but it freaked me out. Then the next morning I woke up and there was a black feather on the pillow next to me. It must have caught in my hair when the bird flew into me, that's all. But still.'

'But you were OK,' said Ash. 'Nothing bad happened.'

Dad laughed. 'No, but it nearly did.'

'What?'

'Something and nothing. It was a couple of weeks later, during the Stag Chase. I was the stag boy and I took a route along the length of Stag's Leap. Then...well, have you ever had that feeling that your body is intent on doing something even though your mind is screaming "no"?'

'Yeah,' said Ash. 'I think so, a couple of times.'

'Well, it was that. I found myself standing at the very edge of the Leap, looking down. I don't even know how I got there. Must have zoned out or something. And my body wanted to launch into the air, to jump. It was such a powerful urge I can even feel it now, just thinking about it. Crazy. So I was standing there, sort of frozen between wanting to jump and knowing I mustn't, and this dread that my body might just do it without my permission. And I wasn't alone. I thought I could see these other boys there, like shadows, only in colour. I don't know what. They were angry, full of hate. Smashing darkness at me. Trying to force me off the edge.'

'But you didn't let them. You were OK.'

'I was OK because Tom Cullen saw me standing there, all freaked out. He grabbed me, hauled me back from the edge. He saved my life. He really did. Then he just ran off and left me to finish the race. So I did. And I won. Except I didn't win really, did I, because Tom had caught up with me and then let me go. I told the organisers but Tom denied it. He never did admit to it. Told me I'd got mountain fever or something and that I'd imagined the whole thing.'

Dad looked straight ahead, his expression hidden by the dark.

For a moment Ash considered telling him that he'd be the stag boy this year. But Dad was talking to him at last and Ash didn't want him to stop, didn't want to put himself at the centre of the conversation. And maybe he should take Dad's experience as a warning anyway, a sign that there really were dark forces at work in the mountains, just like Mark said, vengeful wraiths set on killing stag boys. Mark. He remembered the note Mark had left taped to his bedroom window. Perhaps he should take everything more seriously and do what Mark wanted, pull out of the race, stay at home, stay safe.

'Strange things happen sometimes, Dad,' he said.

'Yeah, I suppose they do,' said Dad. 'When I was out in the desert, I kept coming back to that day up on Stag's Leap. I don't know why. I hadn't thought about it in years, then suddenly I couldn't get it out of my mind. Seems like everywhere I go I'm surrounded by angry ghosts. They came for me all those years ago and now they're coming for me again.'

'But we'll be OK, won't we, Dad? We'll get through all this.'

'I hope so.'

Then Dad fell silent again and they crossed the fields in cold moonlight. Half-formed questions drifted through Ash's mind but he was too tired now to ask them. His eyes half closed. Feet dragging. He yawned, longed for his bed and sleep. Dad put his arm around his shoulders and they trudged home, side by side.

FOURTEEN

It was daylight when Ash woke. He checked the alarm clock. Gone nine o'clock already. Up too late last night trailing Dad around the mountains and now he'd over-slept, messed up his training schedule for the day. He rolled out of bed, pulled on his clothes, hurtled down the stairs two at a time.

He stopped in his tracks in the kitchen door-way. Dad was in there, standing by the cooker. Fully dressed, clean-shaven, making scrambled eggs and toast. A fresh bandage on his injured hand. He still looked thin and tired but otherwise he seemed almost his old self.

'Morning,' said Dad. 'Do you want some breakfast?'

Ash hardly dared reply in case his words broke what-ever spell had brought Dad back to life. 'Yeah,' he said at last. 'Thanks, Dad.' He glanced across the kitchen.

Next to the back door stood a small rucksack and a couple of fishing rods sheathed in canvas.

Dad saw him looking and smiled as he set down two plates of eggs on the table. 'I thought we could go out fishing today,' he said. 'Unless you've got other plans.'

Mark's note, summoning Ash to his camp in the wood. *Or I'll find you . . .*

Ash hesitated for a heartbeat. 'No,' he said. 'I mean, no, I haven't got any other plans. Yes to fishing. Fishing sounds great.' He sat down opposite Dad. 'Where's Mum? Isn't she up yet?'

'Yeah. She's gone out. Visiting Harry, I think.'

Harry, short for Harriet. Mum's closest friend in Thornditch, a booming woman in her sixties who lived in a tumbledown cottage at the other end of the village.

'Harriet!' said Ash. 'I'm amazed she hasn't called round since you got back.'

'She probably has,' said Dad. 'I know Mr King next door came round yesterday morning. I heard his voice. Mum sent him away. I don't think I'm allowed visitors at the moment. Probably for the best.'

'I thought Mum would be here with you,' said Ash. 'Now you're up and about.'

Dad gave a wry smile. 'I think she's had enough of me lately.'

They finished their breakfasts. Dad made a stack of untidy ham sandwiches, filled a Thermos flask with coffee and a plastic bottle with tap water. Ash loaded everything into the rucksack.

'Pike Tarn all right?' said Dad.

The other side of Tolley Carn, and where they used to go when Ash was a kid. A cold clear mountain lake, sunlight burning through mist rising off the water, the eerie calls of curlews. 'Yeah,' said Ash. 'Pike Tarn would be good.'

They set off up the lane. Sun beating off the road surface. Where the lane hooked around the ruins of an ancient barn, they stopped to stare at the leathery remains of a frog, flattened by a passing car and sundried to a perfect cut-out version of itself.

'You tried to eat one of these once,' said Dad.

Ash laughed. 'I never did.'

'Aye, you did. You were about two, I think. You peeled it right off the lane and your mum just got it away from you before you started chewing on it like a liquorice bootlace.'

'Ugh,' said Ash. 'Gross. Best I don't remember that.'

'Do you remember the last time we came out here?' said Dad. 'When we slept out under the stars.'

'Yeah,' said Ash. Laughed again. 'And we didn't bring

any food with us because you said we'd catch our own supper. But we didn't catch anything.'

'I'd forgotten about that part.'

'You had to blag food off those campers.'

'Baked beans and macaroni, aye. Delicious!'

'We were that hungry by then even a squashed frog would have been delicious.'

They didn't mention last night, the long walk up to Stag's Leap and the Cullen farm and back.

They left the lane. They followed the footpath past a row of wind-twisted thorn trees up the lower slopes of Tolley Carn. Then, in the valley below, there was a wink of dazzling light.

Dad flinched and shouted out. He grabbed Ash's wrist, hauled him behind the cover of the nearest thorn tree, pushed him down to the ground.

They crouched there.

The seesaw of Dad's breathing, quick and raw.

'What?' said Ash. He was trembling, couldn't stop. 'What is it, Dad?'

Dad's breathing slowed, steadied. He gave a sharp laugh. Shook his head. 'That flash of light down in the valley,' he said.

'Yeah,' said Ash. 'I saw it. It was just sunlight catching a car wing mirror or a window or something.'

'I know. I know what it was.'

Ash watched him.

'There were snipers,' said Dad. 'Out in the desert. They'd lie in wait in the dunes or on the rooftops of buildings along the roads. Sometimes the sunlight would flash on their rifle scopes. You learn to dive for cover when you see that. Gets to be second nature after a while.'

'It's OK,' said Ash. 'There aren't any snipers here.'

'I know,' said Dad. He rubbed his hand over his face, drew a long breath. 'I know that. Sorry, lad.'

They stood up, continued along the path. The moment should have passed but it hung on, Dad still edgy, his face glossy with sweat, his eyes scanning the mountainside as if he still half expected snipers to be hiding in the bracken.

'You all right now?' said Ash.

No reply.

Change the subject. Get Dad thinking about something that wasn't snipers and war. But he only had one bit of real news. The Stag Chase. Suddenly his mouth felt dry. After last night, Dad telling him about his own time as the stag boy, the timing seemed all wrong. But he'd have to tell him sooner or later anyway. Dad was up and about now, and in a small place like Thornditch, nothing stayed secret for long.

'I'm running in this year's Stag Chase,' he said. The words racing out. 'I won the trials last month. I'm going to be the stag boy. It's official.'

Silence.

'Dad?'

Nothing. It was as if he hadn't spoken.

'Dad? Did you hear what I said?'

'Yeah, I heard,' said Dad. A taut smile on his face. 'That's brilliant news. I'm proud of you.'

'You don't mind? Only after last night...'

'Don't worry about what I said last night. My head's all over the place lately. I knew you were going out running every day and I knew the Stag Chase was coming up, but I've been so caught up in my own problems, I never put two and two together. I'm really sorry. You're a great runner. You'll leave them in the dust.'

'But the things you said, about when you were the stag boy. About wanting to jump off the edge of the Leap and Tom Cullen saving your life. Maybe it's a bad idea. Maybe I shouldn't run.'

'That was twenty years ago,' said Dad. 'Twenty Stag Chases ago. There are always stories about strange goings-on at the Stag Chase. A bit like Halloween, I suppose.'

'But you said you saw things yourself out there on the

Leap when you were the stag boy. Shadowy figures, ghosts. That black feather.'

'Yeah, well, like I said, it was a long time ago. I've seen a lot of things since then, good things and terrible things. And right now what I'd most like to see is you out there, running like the wind.' He smiled. 'Maybe you can put the ghosts to rest for me.'

Ash laughed. 'I'll try. Will you come then, watch the race?'

'Of course I will.'

They trudged up the last stretch to the summit, a crown of burned grass studded with rough grey rock. Beyond, the land fell away steeply to the eastern shore of Pike Tarn.

Dad stopped at the top of the path. He shrugged off the rucksack. Then he just stood there, staring wide-eyed at the lake as if the mouth of hell had just yawned open before him. Suddenly he was sweating and tense again.

'Dad,' said Ash. 'What's wrong?'

No answer.

'Dad?'

'Shut up,' said Dad. Taking quick, shallow breaths. Still staring down towards the lake.

Ash followed his gaze. No flash of sunlight this time. Nothing out there except a raven flapping over the tarn towards them, rough cries grating from its open beak.

'What is it, Dad? There's nothing there. Is it the bird? The raven?'

And it must have been, because there was only the bird, feathers black and glossy as oil, and Dad's gaze fixed on it as it flew closer.

The raven arced above them, veered away.

'I can't do this,' said Dad. 'I'm sorry. I'm not ready. I can't do it.'

He pushed past Ash, set off back down the path at a stumbling run.

Ash took off after him. 'Wait! Dad! What's wrong?'

'Nothing,' said Dad. Breathing hard, his eyes full of panic and a strange sort of anger. 'Everything. Home. I need to go home.'

Ash followed. Words tumbled from him. 'Dad, stop. We're here, Dad, on Tolley Carn. It's OK. Everything's all right. The lake's just there. We'll go down and do some fishing like we planned. Dad! Please, Dad.'

Dad's voice came back to him, raw and desperate. 'Leave me alone, Ash. Stop following me!'

Ash stopped. He watched his dad go, running and stumbling back down to the lane and along it until he was lost to the distance.

Ash crouched in a patch of shade thrown by a thorn tree. Head in his hands, blinking away tears. He felt sick inside. The last thing he wanted to do now was trail back along the path in Dad's wake to the silent house, the closed doors, the tension that never seemed to go away.

He stood up. There was still the whole day ahead of him. Briefly he thought about going to Mark's camp, like Mark wanted him to. But he wasn't in the mood for Mark's craziness, not right now. To hell with him, and to hell with Dad.

He walked back up to the summit and picked up the rucksack and fishing rods where Dad had dropped them.

On the far shore of the lake, there were boys diving from the rocks. Their distant voices and laughter echoed across the water. Careless, carefree. Lads from school, most likely, but they were too far away for him to see their faces. A year ago, he and Mark might have been with them, diving down into the deep dark water until their lungs felt about to burst, then kicking upwards again towards the bright shimmer of sunlight on the surface.

A sudden loneliness hollowed him. He didn't make friends easily. He was too skinny and too intense, the sort of kid bullies gravitate to. Not a fighter like Dad. Or like Mark. But Mark had always been there, ever since Ash could remember, and no one messed with Mark so no one messed with Ash either. But now Mark was gone to the wild, and none of the other boys would hang out with Ash until after the Stag Chase. He was the stag boy and they were the hounds and that was just how things were now until after the race.

He had no one. There was nothing to hold on to any more except the Stag Chase, and even that felt like it was slipping away from him, with its dark history unfolding and Mark telling him not to run.

He slithered untidily down the steep slope. A mini landslide of loose stones bounced down ahead of him, but the diving boys were too far off to notice.

On the narrow shingle beach that bracketed the lake, he set down the rucksack and stripped to his underpants. He waded, then swam out and floated on his back.

Swallows skimmed the water for insects.

Underneath him stretched the great depth of lake and mountain, the Earth turning under cloudless heights of sky.

And he was a speck drifting, shoreless.

FIFTEEN

He sat on a rock and let the sun dry his skin and hair. He watched the distant boys larking about at the water's edge. He ate some of the sandwiches Dad had made, washed them down with bottled water. Then he pulled on his shorts, his walking boots and T-shirt, hooked the rucksack over his shoulders. He scrambled back up the slope to the top of Tolley Carn.

Below him to the east lay Thornditch.

To the south, Carrog Ridge and beyond that the lane that ran around to the Monks Bridge and then towards Mark's camp.

High on Carrog Ridge stood a solitary figure, motionless, silhouetted against the pale sky.

The hairs on the back of Ash's neck prickled. Then the figure lifted one arm, waved, gestured as if it wanted him to come across to it.

Dad or Mark. But he knew it wasn't Dad. Dad would be at home by now, shut in his dark room again. So it had to be Mark.

Or I'll find you, Mark had said in his note. And he had found him.

For a moment, Ash hesitated. He could just walk away, keep his head down, focus on his running for the last few days before the Stag Chase.

But he needed more answers, and Mark was the only one who could give them.

He set off towards the ridge.

The raven returned from the other side of the lake, a black rag flapping across a pale sky. Its soft honking call sounded above him for a while, then the bird flew off. Just a regular bird. Nothing sinister, nothing mysterious.

Mark was still there on the high ground, still watching him when he came to the narrow valley on the southern side of Tolley Carn. Mark raised his arm again and pointed in the direction of his woodland camp. Then he dropped down below the skyline, out of sight.

Ash walked through knee-high grass as dry as tinder. Butterflies flopped in the windless air. A pair of buzzards circled lazily high above him. He reached the lane and followed it around the foot of Carrog Ridge to the Monks Bridge and beyond. Then he took the route Callie had shown him to the woods where Mark was camped.

He stepped from the hot glare of sunlight into cool shadow.

The bone faces watched him with their sightless eyes.

Around them, the woods were gloomy and silent. No sign of Mark anywhere, except for the sheep skulls.

Somewhere above the leaf canopy, a buzzard mewed.

The campfire in the clearing was a patch of cold white ash and a few charred sticks. Around it, the tall grass and nettles were broken and crushed as if a dozen or more people had trampled through.

There was something else. A trace of wood smoke in the air. The iron stink of blood.

He looked down.

Rusty flecks spattered on grass and fern. A small pool of blood on the ground, blackish red and glossy. He crouched, touched the tip of his forefinger to its surface.

It was still tacky.

Whether it was animal or human blood, he couldn't tell. Either seemed possible.

He remembered the venison Mark had cooked on the fire. Maybe that's all it was, blood spilled from another gutted deer.

He crossed the clearing.

A breeze stirred the leaves.

Now he could smell more than just blood and wood smoke. A sickly sweet, rotten stench filled the air. Flies and wasps stormed under the trees. He swatted them away.

He looked around. Looked up.

A stag carcass hung from a branch above, swinging in the breeze. Its head was gone, hacked off. Maggots bulged and gleamed in the blackened gore at its neck.

Ash covered his nose and mouth with one hand, tried not to breathe. His stomach heaved.

There was a movement in the bushes beyond the carcass. A flash of white and red. Laughter.

'Ash,' called a voice. As soft as the breeze through the leaves. 'Over here!'

'Mark,' said Ash. Heart thumping. 'Stop messing around.'

More laughter.

'Over here,' said the voice. Louder this time. Closer, somewhere to the side now.

Ash turned.

A figure came through the trees. Sackcloth mask, scabby with dried clay. Ragged mouth, eyeholes that seemed to have nothing but shadows behind them.

Not tall enough to be Mark.

Now more hound boys approached behind the first.

Ash turned but they were all around him, coming from all sides, closing in. No way out. Mark had lured him into a trap.

The hound boys came closer. Their dry, clay-crusted skin pressed against him. The scent of blood came from them, hot and metallic. Their whispering voices were as scratchy as the wind in dead grass, and as senseless. He couldn't tell if they were flesh and blood or the ghosts he'd seen up on the Leap nearly a week and a half ago.

They wrenched the rucksack from his shoulders.

That felt real enough.

'Hey, that's mine,' he said. He grabbed at it, missed. 'Give it here!'

Boys from school, he told himself. That was all. Boys tormenting him because he was the stag boy, because Mark had put them up to it. They'd rough him up a bit, try to scare him, and that would be that.

Still, his heart raced with fear.

The hound boys laughed behind their masks. They passed the rucksack back through their ranks and closed in tighter.

One of them scooped up a handful of ash from the cold remains of the campfire. He threw it in Ash's face, rubbed it into his skin and hair. Ash coughed and choked, eyes streaming.

The weight of their bodies bore him forward. They hauled him over a fallen tree poxy with black fungus, across ground ankle deep with ivy, past clumps of bracken and green licks of hart's tongue.

Smoke from a small fire drifted under the leaf canopy. The hounds stopped, gazed into its bright heart. One of them tossed a handful of something into the flames. Smell of burning leaves. Ash's eyes, nose, throat filled with bitter smoke.

They seized him, pushed him down onto the ground. Held down his arms and legs so he couldn't move.

'Be still,' hissed one. 'Be still for the stag god.'

Then the god came.

At first he was a silhouette, a shadow. The afternoon sunlight slanted through the trees behind him, hazy beams, dust motes drifting and sparkling. The god was taller than any of the hound boys. A cloak of black feathers swung about him. Instead of a man's head, a stag's head sat upon his shoulders, crowned with spreading antlers.

The hounds drew back to let him through.

Ash stared up into two dull, dead eyes. The stag's nose and half-open mouth tarry with congealed blood.

The stag god crouched over him. Stench of blood, rotten meat, death.

And the cloak. It was made of bird skins, feathered and bloody, eyeless heads still attached. Steely beaks.

Rooks, like the dead rooks Ash had seen hanging from a branch the last time he'd come here.

The god took a thin, vicious knife from under his cloak. The hand that held it was caked with cracked clay, the colour of rust or dried blood. Black dirt under his fingernails.

'Earth and stone,' whispered the god, 'fire and ash, blood and bone.'

'Mark,' said Ash. His voice shaking. 'I know it's you. I know your voice.'

'Me, and not me. Be still. It will hurt less if you're still.'

Ash tensed, tried to wrench away from the hounds pressing down on him. But there were too many of them, too strong, too heavy. 'What will hurt less?' He couldn't catch his breath. Maybe Mark wasn't going to wait for the Stag Chase. Maybe this was it, the kill, the blood sacrifice that he had threatened. 'Killing me won't bring back your dad,' he said. His voice thin and shaky.

'Hush. Be still.'

The knife descended tip first. Ash felt its cold bite as it broke the skin just below his collarbone. He flinched, bit back a cry. The hounds whooped and hollered and bayed. Then the cold became a white-hot thread of pain that moved this way and that across his chest.

The stag's dead eyes watched without seeing. Ash gazed back through a haze of pain and smoke and blood and terror. A cloud of flies buzzed around the rotting head. Then the knife lifted, vanished back under the cloak of bird skins. Mark straightened and stood. He raised his head and bellowed. Then he turned his back on Ash, walked away through the hound boys, vanished back into the gloom.

Ash sucked in air. A knot of darkness unravelled inside him. The world around him spun away, dimmed and disappeared.

When he opened his eyes again, he was alone.

He sat up. Pain clawed across his chest. Wincing, he got to his feet. His stomach heaved. Bile flooded his mouth. He gagged and spat.

The wood was silent except for the shrill staccato jabber of a startled blackbird.

The fishing rods and the rucksack were on the ground where the hounds had dropped them. He rummaged in the rucksack, found the water bottle, rinsed his mouth, spat, then drank deeply.

A tiny sound, the pop of a twig cracking underfoot.

He looked up.

In the darkness among the trees a shard of sunlight lit up a face. Someone watching him. Then the breeze scattered leaf shadows and the sunlight and the face were gone.

But not before he'd recognised the watcher.

The wild man who'd taken the wolf-dog.

Bone Jack.

SIXTEEN

Ash stood among the trees at the bottom of the drive. He stared up at the house. Most likely Mum was in the back garden but he couldn't count on it. He couldn't let her see him, not pale with ash, his shirt slashed open and his chest all cut up and a mess of blood. She'd freak.

Hidden in the undergrowth, he waited. He watched the house until he was certain Mum wasn't inside and Dad was holed up in his room. Then he loped up the drive to the front door and let himself in.

Silence.

No one around.

Upstairs, he locked the bathroom door behind him. He stood in front of the mirror. Dried blood crusted his chest.

His face was ghostly with the ash the hound boy had thrown at him.

He soaked a facecloth in cold water and squeezed it out over the wounds on his chest, wiped away blood, rinsed the cloth, wiped away more blood.

He looked in the mirror again. Now most of the blood was gone, a pattern was visible: a crude stag's head cut into his flesh, just like the one he'd seen daubed on the stag boy's chest that day on the Leap.

Ash drew a sharp breath. He ran his fingertips over the cuts. The wounds were tender and shallow, not much more than scratches really. They'd hurt for a few days then they'd heal, probably not even leave a scar.

Even so, terror hammered in his chest.

He took slow breaths, forced himself to calm down. There had to be an explanation for it all. The stag god wasn't any sort of god. It was just Mark, wearing a grotesque headdress made of the dead stag's head and a cloak made from bloodied bird skins. Horrific and crazy, but still Mark. And the hound boys were just ordinary boys behind their masks, doing what Mark told them. Somehow Mark had made himself their leader. Because he was cleverer, quicker, stronger, wilder, more charismatic than they were. Because he was mad and his madness made him powerful.

Just boys. It was all just boys. Nothing supernatural. They were playing mind games, trying to intimidate him. The hounds always intimidated the stag boy before the race, he reminded himself. It was expected.

Everything was OK.

But it didn't feel OK. It felt dark, dangerous. There was death all around it. The stag's head, all those rooks. Mark must have caught them somehow, maybe netted them or shot them down with a catapult. And then he'd killed them, skinned them, made them into that cloak. It was sick, wrong.

Ash wished he could talk to Dad about it all, ask him if he knew what all this stuff meant, ask him what he should do. But Dad was lost in his own nightmares. He couldn't handle Ash's terrors as well.

Ash's head ached with it all.

He showered, washed away the last traces of blood and the bitter smell of smoke that clung to his skin and hair. He found the first-aid box that Mum kept in the bathroom cupboard. He smeared antiseptic cream over the wounds and taped dressings over the top. Then he wrapped himself in a huge towel and crept upstairs to his bedroom on the top floor. Still no sign of Mum and Dad anywhere. He stuffed the bloodied T-shirt and facecloth into a corner at the back of the wardrobe, dressed himself in clean clothes.

Everything hidden, everything as ordinary as he could make it.

He lay on his bed. Sunlight played across the ceiling. His body felt empty, a shell. He floated above it, half asleep, far away from everything. Dad downstairs in his room, his head full of demons. Mum out in the garden, herself and yet not herself.

Lies. Secrets. Blood and death. None of it made any sense. He didn't know any more if the world had gone mad or if he had.

He turned his head, gazed out of the window. Unblinking.

He needed to find Callie. She was the only person he could think of who might understand any of this. The only person who might know what Mark was doing and might be able to make him stop.

Tomorrow though.

Callie could wait until tomorrow. The world could wait.

He was weary to the bone. He closed his eyes and let sleep take him.

SEVENTEEN

Next morning he walked to the high street and caught the bus to Coldbrook. A couple of lads from his year at school were horsing around on seats at the back. Liam Tunney and Chris Brooker. They shot glances at him. They whispered and sniggered. 'Dead man walking,' said Brooker loudly. They both laughed.

Ash stayed away from them. He sat near the front, among the pensioners on their way to Coldbrook's shops and cafes. He felt the boys' eyes on him, heard their voices and laughter but he didn't look round. They'd be hound boys, he knew. Almost every local youth between the ages of fifteen and twenty would be a hound boy in the Stag Chase. So they'd probably been there yesterday too, in the wood with the other boys, their faces hidden behind masks, holding Ash down while Mark carved the stag's head into Ash's chest.

He wondered how much else they knew. They could be in on everything, part of Mark's plan to kill the stag boy and bring back his dad from the dead.

He pushed the thought aside. He was just being paranoid. Brooker and Tunney were thugs, that was all. Mark wouldn't trust them with anything important.

Beyond the window, the trees lining the lane gave way to dry-stone walls and patchwork fields, then the rough open moors of the uplands. The bus crested a hill and now Coldbrook filled the valley below, a sprawl of tightly packed houses rising in tiers up the lower slopes of the mountains to either side.

One of those houses belonged to Grandpa Cullen.

Ash had been there once before, with Mark. But that was a long time ago and all he remembered was a few worn steps leading from the pavement to a green front door. A whitewashed terraced house. A curve of railing. A fiery orange geranium in a flowerpot.

Where though? The only parts of town Ash knew well were the high street and the bus route to his school. But there were so many other streets, so many houses. They all looked alike.

He got off the bus in the town centre. Liam Tunney and Chris Brooker got off too. They cackled like hyenas and elbowed each other as they passed him. He hung back, watched them head off along the high street until they disappeared into the crowd.

Cars, shoppers, music blaring from a clothes shop, a streak of kids pelting past on BMX bikes. The rush of noise and movement made him giddy. He walked along the high street until it split into three at a roundabout. Then he walked back again, wandered down a cobbled side street that swung sharply to the left then ended abruptly at a high brick wall mottled and veined with faded blue graffiti.

He retraced his steps to the high street, at a loss. He stopped at a corner, turned this way and then that, wondering what to do, where to go. Without the name of the road Grandpa Cullen lived on, he couldn't even ask for directions or look at a map.

'You look lost, lad,' said a voice. Two elderly women, smiling kindly at him. They both looked old enough to have been at school with Grandpa Cullen.

'I'm looking for my friend's grandpa's house,' he said. 'Only I can't remember where it is.'

'What's his name?' said one of the women. 'We've lived here all our lives. We might know him.'

'Cullen,' said Ash. 'Mr Cullen.'

'George Cullen,' said the woman, looking at the other. 'He must mean George Cullen.'

'Must do,' agreed the second woman.

'Pocket Lane, I think,' said the first woman. 'Is that right? Or is it Harper Lane?'

'Pocket Lane,' said the other. 'Definitely Pocket Lane.' They directed Ash towards the north side of town. Third row of houses beyond the church spire, or was it the fourth row. Somewhere around there anyway.

'I can't tell you what number house, mind,' said the first woman. 'You'll have to ask someone else when you get there.'

'I will,' said Ash. 'Thanks.'

Pocket Lane. He recognised it as soon as he saw it, though it was narrower than he remembered and the houses were smaller and grubbier. Grandpa Cullen's whitewashed house stood out among the dark grey stone and pebbledash. There were the steps up to it, the railing, the green door. The potted geranium was gone. The windows were dark.

He rang the doorbell and waited.

Nothing.

He rang it a second time, then hammered the brass knocker for good measure. Still nothing. He leaned over the railing and peered through the living-room window. No one there, just a fireplace, a couple of heavy old armchairs, a coffee table with a folded newspaper and a stack of unopened letters on top of it, a TV set in the far corner. He drew back and knocked on the front door again.

A neighbour came out from next door. A large middle-aged woman with honey-coloured hair, her rolled sleeves exposing powerful forearms. A cold, suspicious expression on her heavy face. 'Can I help you?' she said.

'Is this where Grandpa Cullen lives?' he said. 'George Cullen?'

Her eyes narrowed. 'What do you want with Mr Cullen?'

'It's not him exactly. I'm looking for Callie, his granddaughter.'

'What do you want with Callie then?'

'It's personal.'

She stared at him, stone-faced.

'I just want to ask her where her brother is,' he said. 'Mark. I know him from school. He was my best mate.'

'Was?'

'We fell out.'

'Ah. And now you want to make up with him, do you?' The woman's expression softened a little. 'They're not here, love.'

'It's OK. I'll wait.'

'They're not coming back. No one lives there now.

George fell sick and went into hospital a month ago. He couldn't look after himself, never mind take care of two children. Not that it was much of a surprise. His health's not been good for years. I don't suppose he'll last much longer, bless him.'

She paused. Then: 'You know about his son, I suppose. The children's father.'

Ash nodded. 'Yeah.'

A clap of wings overhead. Ash flinched and glanced up. Just a pigeon, launching from the chimney stack. And a face at the upstairs window, Callie's face. She pressed a finger to her lips and drew back into the gloom inside.

'Jumpy lad, aren't you?' said the woman.

'The pigeon,' he said vaguely. 'It startled me, that's all.'

'Anyway,' she said, 'where was I?'

'Mr Cullen's health.'

'Ah yes.' She sighed theatrically. 'That terrible business with his son. I think that was the last straw. Broke his heart, it did. Anyway, the children went off to stay with relatives in Thornditch, so I was told. I expect Mr Cullen's house will be up for sale soon.'

Thornditch. They didn't have any relatives there. They didn't have any relatives anywhere that Ash knew of, except for Grandpa Cullen. And now he knew that Callie was in the house anyway, hiding upstairs. Maybe she'd been secretly staying there all along.

'OK,' said Ash. 'Thanks. Sorry for bothering you.'

The woman smiled. 'It's no bother, love. If you ask around Thornditch, I'm sure you'll find them soon enough. It's only a little village. Someone will know.'

'Right,' said Ash. 'I will. Thanks.'

'What's your name, love? So I can pass it on if I see anyone.'

'Ash,' he said. 'Ash Tyler.'

'Tyler? Stephen Tyler's lad?'

A hard edge in her voice now. She knew who his dad was. Ash should have kept his mouth shut.

'Don't you live in Thornditch?' she said.

'No,' he said. Reddening at the lie. Forcing a smile, backing away. 'Must be a different Tyler.'

He walked away slowly, told himself it probably didn't matter. The woman didn't know anything much. Didn't know Mark was living wild in the mountains. Didn't even know that Callie was staying in Grandpa Cullen's house.

But she'd known he'd lied, he was certain of it, and now she'd realise that Mark and Callie couldn't be in Thornditch. What if she started snooping?

And he still needed to talk to Callie.

He looked back. The neighbour was standing in the middle of the pavement, her arms folded, watching him go.

He felt her gaze on him all the way to the end of the street.

EIGHTEEN

In the end, it was Callie who found him. As he headed back towards the town centre, she must have hurried along the back lanes to catch up with him and suddenly there she was, walking out of an alley of broken stone and fireweed.

'I saw you,' he said. 'At the upstairs window.'

She walked beside him with her head bent, looking at the ground.

'Have you been living there?' he said. 'All this time? On your own?'

'I don't exactly live there. It's too risky. I go there to get food and change my clothes. Sometimes I spend the night there. I sneak in round the back after dark so Mrs Hopkinson won't see me. I don't turn on the lights or make any noise and I keep away from the windows.'

'Is that the nosy neighbour? She thought you were staying with relatives in Thornditch.'

'That's what Mark told her.'

'Why?'

She shot him a strange look, half annoyed and half pitying. 'Because we're alone. There isn't anyone to look after us, not now Grandpa's in hospital. Mark's OK, he's sixteen, but I'm only fourteen and they'd take me into care if they knew.'

'Right,' he said. Face hot with embarrassment. 'I think I've dropped you in it. I think your neighbour knows that I'm from Thornditch and she's figured out that you can't be living there as well, otherwise I'd have known about it. I'm sorry.'

Callie chewed her lip. 'It's OK,' she said at last. 'She'd probably have found out anyway, sooner or later. It's better this way than if she'd just seen me sneaking in one night and called the police or social services. At least now I know to steer clear. Why did you come to the house anyway?'

'I was looking for you. I thought you might know more about what Mark's up to.'

'He's still camping in that wood, as far as I know.'

'Yeah, I saw him there yesterday but that's not what I mean.'

'What, then?'

He looked away. He didn't want to tell her about his encounter with Mark and the hound boys, Mark wearing the dead stag's head and a cloak of dead birds. Not yet. Maybe never. 'I don't know,' he said. 'He's acting really weird. I don't understand anything he says any more.'

Callie laughed. 'And you think I do?'

They walked along in silence for a while, back on the high street now, voices and clatter and colour and movement, the air stale with exhaust fumes.

'Where do you sleep when you don't go to your grandpa's house?' said Ash.

She shrugged. 'Out in the mountains, here and there.'

'Don't you have friends you could stay with?'

'Yeah, a few. But if I stay with them, there'll be questions, and next thing there'll be social workers involved and I could end up anywhere, miles away. So I avoid my friends. It's easier that way.'

'Suppose they see you around? Like now, walking down the street?'

She gave a strange little smile. 'When your mum's dead and your dad's hanged himself and your brother's gone feral, your friends suddenly stop making much effort to be around you.'

'Aren't you afraid, alone out in the mountains at night?'

'I've lived in the mountains all my life. Of course I'm not afraid of them.'

'Maybe you should be,' he said darkly. 'There's things out there.'

'What things?'

Your lunatic brother, he thought. Ghosts, Bone Jack . . . The words hung in his mind, unspoken.

'What things?' said Callie again.

Before he could answer, footsteps closed in behind them, then Ash felt a heavy arm across his shoulders. A freckled, sunburned face glossed with sweat pushing towards his. Grinning, breath that smelled of burger and ketchup. Chris Brooker. Liam Tunney just a pace or two behind him.

Ash shoved Brooker away.

Brooker flung up his hands in mock surrender. 'Whoa there, soldier boy! I'm just being friendly. I heard about your dad. Heard they had to send him home because he'd gone nuts.' Still grinning, his eyes hard.

'What do you want?' said Ash. Backing away.

'Just wanted to see how you are, like I said. Soldier boy, stag boy. How's that carving on your chest? Healing up nicely?'

Ash took another step back, and another. He glanced across at Callie. She was staring at Chris Brooker as if she wanted to punch him.

'Earth and stone,' hissed Brooker, 'fire and ash, blood and bone.'

Ash grabbed Callie's wrist. 'Run,' he said. 'Just run!'

So they ran, dodging along the crowded pavement, between shoppers who swung wide-eyed faces at them like startled cattle.

Behind them, laughter, fast footfalls, angry passers-by yelling.

'This way,' said Callie. Pulled him with her across a courtyard then into a crowded cafe and out through open glass doors to a terraced garden. An old man staring at them, cup of tea stalled midway to his lips. Two women, a baby squalling in a pram. Ash twisted his body around the pram, muttered, 'Sorry, sorry.' Past a tortoiseshell cat curled up in the sunshine and out through a rickety green door onto a narrow back lane that smelled of rotting cabbage. He followed Callie along a snicket between two garages to another lane and then another where they stopped to catch their breath, crouching among tall weeds beside a stone wall. The cuts on Ash's chest felt tight and hot and sore under the dressings. He looked down at his chest, half expecting to see blood seeping through his T-shirt, but there was nothing.

'That sweaty boy,' said Callie. 'What did he say? That stuff about earth and blood or whatever it was?'

'Earth and stone, fire and ash, blood and bone.'

'What does that mean? Why did it make you run?'

'I don't know,' said Ash. 'I've heard it before though. I heard Mark say it yesterday.'

'What exactly went on that made you come and find me?'

'Mark...' He paused, wondering how much to tell her. 'He left a note for me, telling me to meet him. I didn't go but he found me out in the mountains and I followed him back to his camp in the woods. All the hound boys were waiting for me there. Mark must have set it up, I suppose. Then he came out dressed as the stag god.'

She shot him a sideways look. 'Dressed as the what?'

He didn't answer right away.

'Tell me,' she said. 'I can't take any more of people not telling me things. My dad was like that before he killed himself. Now Mark. I've had enough of it. I know Mark is into some strange stuff so I don't care if you tell me something weird or bad. I'm ready for that. Just tell me.'

Dark memories played through Ash's mind. Knife and blood, the severed stag's head, the stink of rotting meat.

He didn't want to tell her about those things. They were too bleak, too horrifying.

But she had a right to know. So he started to talk and the words tumbled out, jumbled and urgent, a chaotic stream of consciousness. He told her all of it, not just the stuff about Mark but about Dad as well. She didn't stop him, just crouched by the wall, listening, frowning. He described the weird Stag Chase he'd seen up on the Leap and the shadows that raced along behind him afterwards. He told her about Mark's threats to kill him if he ran as the stag boy, about the raggedy man in the mountains whom Mark had called Bone Jack, and about the wolf-dog, and about Mark as the stag god, and even about the stag's head that he'd carved on Ash's chest. He told her about Dad freaking out and the black feather and the bloody handprint on the window and the sheep skull, Mark trying to push Dad over the edge into madness, trying to scare Ash into pulling out of the Stag Chase.

He told her everything and then he waited.

NINETEEN

Callie was quiet for a long while, staring ahead at nothing. His heart sank.

'Callie—'

'Shut up,' she said. 'I'm thinking. It's a lot to process.'

So he shut up, tilted his head back and watched a gull cut silvery arcs against the pale sky. Nerves fluttered in his stomach.

'I know where he got some of this stuff from,' she said at last. 'Grandpa and Dad used to tell us stories about Bone Jack and the Stag Chase. I used to think they were just folk tales and ghost stories, a bit like fairy tales only rougher and scarier. But I've seen things too, out in the mountains. Those hound boys you said you saw in the woods with Mark, were they boys from school?'

'The ones in the woods yesterday were just local boys, I'm sure of it. The weird hound boys look different, almost solid but not quite, like mirages or something. I saw them that day up on Stag's Leap, just before I saw you.'

She nodded, solemn. 'I saw them too.'

'You told me you didn't. I knew you were lying.'

'I was angry with you.'

'And now you're not?'

'A bit. Not so much.'

'Did you see where they went after they ran past me?'

She shook her head. 'They vanished, like you said. They just sort of dissolved into nothing. Like mist does when the sun gets hot.'

'Ghosts.' Such a little word, a word that sounded almost like a whisper, but saying it out loud and seriously to another person somehow changed everything.

'Maybe.'

'I don't even believe in ghosts,' said Ash. 'Not really. I keep thinking there must be a rational explanation for everything, even if I don't know what it is. Like the bird that flew into me. That could happen, right? A bird could accidentally fly into someone.'

'I suppose so.'

'But it happened to my dad when he was the stag boy. A black bird – a crow or a rook or something – flew into him as well. He saw something up on the Leap too.

145

Shadowy figures, he said. And they got into his head somehow, made him want to jump from the Leap. Your dad saved him. Did you know that?'

'No,' she said softly. 'I didn't know that.'

'Then there's the Stag Chase we saw,' said Ash. 'And the lightning-fast raggedy man, Bone Jack. No one moves that fast. It's not possible. I looked him up online and Bone Jack is a mythic figure, from ancient times, so how can he possibly be real and living in the mountains right now? It's impossible. But I can't explain all of it away, no matter how hard I try. Things happen that I know can't happen in the real world but they keep happening right in front of me anyway. And Mark's in the middle of everything somehow. It always comes back to Mark or the Stag Chase or Bone Jack.'

'What did Mark say about it all?'

Ash shrugged. 'Just what I already told you. He's mad at me. That's fine. I let him down and he's still angry. I get that. But then the next minute he'll be like the old Mark again, like he's still my best mate. Then he'll come out with all this crazy stuff, about Bone Jack and the old ways and sacrifices to the land, telling me not to run in the Stag Chase because this year the stag boy is going to be killed. Killed by him. And I think some of the things he's done, freaking out my dad and then the stag-god stuff in the woods, all that's just to scare me so I won't run.'

'Do you think he means it? About killing the stag boy?'

'I don't know. He's so crazy right now that anything is possible.'

Callie fell silent again.

'I'm sorry,' said Ash.

'Maybe you should do what he says and pull out of the Stag Chase.'

'I've thought about it. But I can't.'

'Can't, or won't?'

He smiled. 'Is there a difference?'

'Yeah, there is.'

'If I pull out, I'll have wasted all that training. I'll be running away from trouble again, like I did when your dad died and I ran out on Mark. If I'd stuck around, he might not have got so crazy. He might have been OK.'

'This might not be the best time to get a guilt complex.'

'Maybe it is. Maybe it's exactly the best time.'

'I think Mark's got what your dad's got,' said Callie. 'Post-traumatic stress. Only Mark got it after he found our dad hanging in the barn.'

'It was Mark who found him?'

'Yes.'

'I didn't know that. He never told me. Why didn't he tell me?'

'He couldn't talk about it. Never has talked about it. I only know because I was there and he came running into the house, yelling that I had to get up, phone for an ambulance. I wanted to go into the barn, see for myself, but he wouldn't let me. He kept hold of me and he wouldn't let me go. He protected me.'

'I didn't know he'd found him.'

He waited for her to get angry again, to tell him not knowing everything was his own fault for running out on Mark. But instead she just stood up and said, 'Come on.'

'Where to?'

'The library,' she said. She smiled. 'Have you ever been to a library?'

He gave her a withering look. 'Yes. But not for a long time. Why are we going there?'

'Because maybe we can find out more,' she said. 'It's all ancient, isn't it? It's all about history. Bone Jack, the ghost hound boys, the wolf-dog you found . . . it's all got something to do with the Stag Chase. I don't know how it all fits together but there must be some connection. So we need to find out more about the Stag Chase, then maybe we'll understand what's going on.'

'I suppose so,' said Ash, uneasy.

'Anyway, it's worth a try,' she said.

'Yeah, I guess.'

He smiled and she frowned back at him. 'Why are you smiling?'

He shrugged. 'I don't know. Because I told you everything, I suppose. Because you believed me, straight away, no questions.'

She sighed. 'Come on, let's go.'

They went through the back lanes, in case Brooker and Tunney were still prowling the high street.

'You and Mark always used to mess around on your bikes,' said Callie. 'Bombing downhill and bashing yourselves up mostly. You never used to go running, but now it seems like it's all you do.'

Ash laughed. 'Yeah, running pretty much is all I do lately.'

'It's important to you, isn't it? The Stag Chase.'

'Yeah, it is. My dad was the stag boy once. Now it's me.'

'Keeping the tradition going then.'

'I suppose, but it's not just that.' He hesitated, suddenly unsure of himself. 'When I'm running, it's like...like the Earth turns under my feet and I'm at the centre of everything, holding everything together. And I have this idea that I can hold Dad together too. I don't know how. It's just a feeling. More than a feeling. Like an instinct or something. That if I run in the Stag Chase and I win then Dad will be OK.' He laughed. 'Sounds crazy, doesn't it?'

'A bit. But maybe it's not.' She stopped. 'We're here.'

TWENTY

Coldbrook Public Library: a big, square building made of pale stone. Ash gazed up at it as he followed Callie towards the door. Maybe she was right and they'd find what they wanted to know, bits and pieces in dusty, long-forgotten books, obscure local histories, old documents, things that were nowhere to be found on the internet.

Inside, the library was cool, airy and quiet. The librarian, a dark-haired man in his thirties, smiled at them as they passed the checkout desk. There was a woman browsing the gardening section, another flicking through a book with a creepy clown's face on the cover, an old man reading a newspaper at a table. Ash and Callie wandered past shelves of crime novels, romance, science fiction, horror.

'Where do we start looking?' said Ash.

'The local history section, I suppose,' said Callie.

'Where's that?'

Callie looked around helplessly. 'I don't know. I'll ask.'

She went off, came back with the dark-haired man.

'This is the librarian,' said Callie. 'He's going to show us where to start.'

'This way,' the librarian said. He led them through a labyrinth of shelving units and partitions into a large sunlit room. 'Anything in particular that you're looking for?'

'A history of the Stag Chase,' said Callie.

'We've got one or two, I think,' he said. 'And quite a few books on local folklore and traditions that will probably have a chapter or two about it.'

'Thanks,' said Ash.

The librarian smiled at him. 'Folklore is a special interest of mine. Are you researching a holiday project for school?'

'No,' said Callie. She glanced at Ash. 'He's the stag boy this year. We just wanted to know more about it all. The history and traditions of the Stag Chase, that sort of thing.'

Ash reddened.

'So you're the stag boy!' said the librarian. 'Great! I love the Stag Chase. I go every year to watch. You must have been training hard.'

'Yeah,' said Ash. 'I have.'

'It's a bit like running a marathon, I suppose.'

'Sort of, but it's not as far and no one is timing you so you can take a break or walk some of it instead of running, if you want to. But the hound boys are chasing you too so you have to be either very fast or very stealthy.'

'Well, good luck with it. You'll find a few useful books in the section over by the window. I'll leave you to it. Come and find me if you need any more help.'

'We will,' said Callie. 'Thanks.'

The section wasn't very big, just a couple of shelves with books on everything from haunted houses to a history of the Coldbrook Morris Men. They pulled out the books with the most promising titles. Eight books, all slim, dog-eared, old.

Ash eyed them. 'We don't have to read them all, do we?'

Callie laughed. 'No. Just skim through and read any bits that look useful.'

They sat down at a table. Ash picked up a book and started flicking through it. Ghost stories, strange bits of history, witches turned to stone, legends of giants who lived in caves in the mountains and kicked around boulders as if they were footballs.

'This looks like the best one,' said Callie. '*A History of the Thornditch Stag Chase* by Sybil Ingham. There has to be something useful in this.'

It was more like a pamphlet than a book: thin, with a battered green cloth cover, published in 1910. Callie opened it and turned pages. 'Most of it's about the nineteenth century,' she said. 'There's just a short section at the front about the origins and early history.'

'Better than nothing,' said Ash. 'What does it say?'

She took her time, read it through carefully. Then she pushed the book across the table towards him. 'Read it yourself.'

He read.

> *The earliest known record of the Stag Chase is a reference to boys running in 'Thornditch's Wyld Hunt' in a 13th-century poem. However, some archaeologists suggest that the stag's head carved on a standing stone near Corbie Tor locates the race's origins in the Dark Ages or earlier. According to oral tradition, the Stag Chase was once a form of human sacrifice in which the stag boy, if caught, was killed by the hounds as a blood offering to the gods. If true, this practice was*

*abandoned or outlawed during the Middle
Ages, though local lore has it that occasional
blood sacrifices were still made for some
centuries after.*

'Right,' said Ash. 'The human-sacrifice stuff is more
or less the same as Mark told me, that night you took
me to see him in the woods. What about that bit that
mentions a standing stone with the stag's head carved on
it? I've never even heard of it. Have you? Near Corbie
Tor, the book says. I haven't heard of that either.'

'I'm not sure,' she said. 'I think it may be somewhere
northwest. I bet Mark would know.'

'Is there anything about Bone Jack?'

'I don't know. I only read that section you just read, on
the origins of the Stag Chase. It doesn't mention him
there.'

He turned more pages, skim-reading. Most of the
book was about the Stag Chase in the nineteenth century,
as Callie had said, and most of that consisted of dull lists
of the names of stag boys and notable hounds. But there
were pictures too, pen-and-ink drawings of mountain
scenes, a twisted hawthorn tree, a hare poised at the edge
of a field.

His breath caught in his throat.

Bone Jack.

The floppy wide-brimmed hat, the eyes at once intense and faraway. The gaunt face.

There was no mistaking him.

'That's him,' said Ash. 'That's the man I met in the mountains, the one who was at Mark's camp. But this book is old, really old.'

'Yeah, published in 1910.'

'Over a hundred years ago. But I saw Bone Jack yesterday, in the woods, and he looked exactly like he does in this picture.'

Callie drew a long breath. 'This is all so mad,' she said.

'Yeah, I know. But I really did see him. I've seen him three times. Twice hanging around the woods where Mark's camp is and once when I found the wolf-dog, like I told you. That picture is of him. It's exactly him.'

'Does it say anything about him?'

'A bit. It says the picture is of a hermit who lived wild in the mountains.' He looked up from the book. 'I looked up Bone Jack online. There wasn't much about him, just a bit in an online encyclopedia that said he was a local version of some other mythic figures, wild men who lived in forests with birds and beasts. He's a bit like them. He lives wild. He has the rooks, and that wolf-dog.'

'Was it a wolf or a dog?'

'I don't know. Bone Jack said it was a wolf but I've never seen one in the flesh and it was in such a state anyway, starving and plastered with dried mud. It could have been, I suppose.'

'So where did it come from? There aren't any wild wolves in Britain any more, so if it was a wolf, it must have escaped from somewhere.'

'Yeah, I asked him about that too.'

'What did he say?'

'He didn't really tell me. He just seemed to think it shouldn't have been there at all.'

'OK,' said Callie. 'So let's say there really was a wolf in the mountains, even though wild British wolves died out hundreds of years ago. And there are ghost hound boys out there too. And there's Bone Jack, whom you saw yesterday looking exactly the same as he does in a picture in a book published over a hundred years ago. The wolf and the ghosts and Bone Jack are all ancient, from another time. They shouldn't be here. They should be dead and gone. So why are they here? Why now?'

'I don't know. But it's not just now. I told you, my dad saw things twenty years ago when he was the stag boy.'

'OK. But it doesn't happen every year, does it? Sometimes people tell stories about seeing ghosts up on the mountains, like the stories my dad and grandpa used to tell to me and Mark. But this isn't stories. This is real. So why now?'

'I don't know. It could be something to do with Mark. Maybe he's summoned them.'

'I don't think so. He's crazy but he hasn't got magic powers or anything. He's just my brother. But maybe it's not about powers. Maybe it's about the land and its history.'

'Mark said something like that,' said Ash. 'Something about the land being sick with foot-and-mouth and drought, no sheep in the mountains any more, everything withering and dying. He said that's why the old ways are coming back. The sicker the land is, the stronger its ghosts get, or something.'

'It makes sense, I suppose,' she said. 'Weird crazy ghost-story sense anyway.'

'Ghost sense,' said Ash. He smiled at her. 'So what do we do now?'

'That's it for today, I suppose. Tomorrow I'm going to find Mark. Whatever he's got himself into, I have to get him out of it.'

'I'll come with you.'

She shook her head. 'No. I have to find him on my own.'

'Why? I'm caught up in all of this, too. I want to know what's going on.'

'I know, but he's still angry with you. He might talk to me about it, but he won't do it if you're there.'

Ash scowled but deep down he knew she was right. Mark would put on an act if he was there, make threats, swagger around like he did the night Callie had taken Ash to his camp. 'OK,' he said at last. 'You go. I'll stay away. But promise me you'll tell me exactly what he says.'

'I will. I promise.'

They put the books back on the shelves and stopped to thank the librarian on their way out. 'Did you find what you wanted?' he said.

Ash nodded. 'Yeah, we found out a few things.'

'Good. I expect I'll see you on Sunday at the Stag Chase then. I hope you have a good race, leave the hounds in the dust.'

'Thanks,' said Ash. 'I'll do my best.'

They left the library, walked back to the high street.

Callie stopped. 'I'll head off now. I'll look for Mark in the morning.'

'Where will you stay tonight? You could come back to ours, only—'

'Yeah, your dad. I know. I couldn't stay with you anyway. There'd be too many questions.'

'Where, then?'

'I haven't decided yet. Not back to Grandpa's house. It's too risky now Mrs Hopkinson suspects something. Maybe back to the farm.'

'Your farm?'

She looked away, wouldn't meet his gaze.

'The farm's all boarded up,' he said.

'There's a way in round the back,' she said. 'It's OK, seriously. It was our home.'

'Yeah, I know, but...' He felt cold and sick inside at the thought of her spending nights there, alone in that silent house in the vast mountain darkness, only metres away from where her dad hanged himself. 'It's creepy.'

'I know it's weird,' she said. 'But everything's so weird anyway that it doesn't matter.'

'Callie...' he said. He was about to say that he'd come with her, stay with her so she wouldn't be alone, but she was already backing away from him. Another step, then another, then she turned and was lost in the throng of shoppers.

Ash stood for a few long moments, watching the crowd where she'd disappeared. Then he headed back to the bus stop.

TWENTY~ONE

Midnight. Two more days until the Stag Chase. Ash tossed and turned in his bed, half awake, half dreaming. He dreamed the stag boy was in his bedroom. Clay-daubed skin like cracked stone, charcoal making hollows of his eyes, the dark gash of his mouth. 'Earth and stone,' the stag boy said. Singsong, his voice soft as a breeze, as cold as death's breath. 'Fire and ash, blood and bone.'

Behind the stag boy, shadows gathered. They loomed above him, folded over him like a black wave. A tide of pitiless dark. The boy sank away into it as if he was drowning.

'Wait for me!' said Ash. But his mouth wouldn't open. The words jammed in his throat. He flung off the bedsheet and stumbled across the room to where the stag boy had been. Followed him into the deep darkness.

Then he was pushing through leaf and twig. Underfoot there wasn't carpet any more; instead he walked barefoot on the dry leaf litter of a woodland floor.

No sign of the stag boy. Nothing except the dark shapes of trees, a star-scattered sky, moonlight.

He emerged from among the trees onto a stretch of scrubby, stony land. He stopped and stared. He'd been here before. The shallow, shrunken stream. The thorn trees. Bone Jack's bothy.

The windows were dark. He went closer. A chill wind rattled the bone strings in the doorway. Beyond them, someone or something moved in the gloom.

The face at the window. Pale, blurred.

The quick beat of his own heart, his blood singing in his ears.

He went closer.

No one there.

A movement nearby. Wing beats, then soft footsteps.

Bone Jack stood in front of him. 'You shouldn't be here, lad. Go home.'

Then all of it was gone, blacked out in a blink.

He was standing in his own bedroom, facing the wall.

The cry of an owl in the trees.

He went to the window, looked out.

Below on the lawn stood a silent pack of masked

hound boys. Their heads were tilted upwards. From behind their masks, they watched him.

He stepped back. Crouched down, below the level of the windowsill, crept forward again, peered out around the edge of the curtain.

The hound boys were gone. There was just moonlit grass, the black trees beyond it. Nothing to suggest they'd ever been there.

Shivering, he got back into bed. He thought about Callie, out there alone in the night. He thought about Mark, clay-painted, wearing the stag's head, cloaked in bloodied rook skins. He thought about Dad.

Fear burned through him like a fever. The bedsheets stuck to his sweat-slick skin.

Night crowded in, hot and heavy, pressing down on him. He hardly knew if his eyes were open or closed. The darkness around his bed filled with footsteps, whispers, a rain of leaves falling slowly and silently. Ghosts calling to him and he had to follow, he had to, but he couldn't move. 'Come with us,' they said. 'Come with us.' His body was a dead weight, his chest so tight he could barely draw breath. With a huge effort, he sat up.

Nothing under him except empty darkness, and he was falling. He clawed at empty air, his throat filled with screams.

He hit the rocks hard. Felt his flesh bruise and tear, his bones shatter, the hot rain of his own blood. A hiss of air escaped his lips.

He heard Bone Jack's voice again. 'Go home,' it said. 'Stay home.'

His eyes snapped open.

Daylight. He was lying on his back in his bed, his arms flung out wide, the sheet twisted around his legs.

And leaves in his hair. He sat upright, frantically brushing them away.

A knock at the door, then it opened and Mum came in. 'Ash?' she said. 'Is everything all right?'

He fumbled with the bedsheet, pulling it up to his chin so she wouldn't see the dressings covering the cuts on his chest.

'Yeah, everything's fine,' he said.

His voice thin and scratchy. His skin still so hot. Bits of dead leaf scattered on the bed, on the floor.

'You were yelling,' said Mum. 'And I thought I heard someone else's voice in here with you.'

Ash glanced around the room. Just in case. Mum had heard something, someone. But what? And how? He must have cried out in imitation of Bone Jack's voice, playing Bone Jack's part in his own nightmare. Or else, somehow, Bone Jack had really been here, in the room and in his dreams at the same time. 'There's no one here,' he said. 'It must have been the radio alarm.'

'The radio alarm,' she said. 'Right. But I definitely heard you yell out. Did you have a nightmare or something?'

'Uh, yeah, I suppose I must have.'

'Want to talk about it?'

He shrugged. 'I can't really remember it. I dreamed I was falling.'

'I get those dreams too sometimes.' She crossed the room and opened the curtains wide. Sunlight poured in. She didn't seem to notice the dead leaves on the floor. 'Lots of people do. It's something to do with going to sleep too quickly and your mind and your body getting out of sync. It feels like you're falling, then you jerk awake again.'

'Sounds right.'

She sat on the edge of his bed and pressed her cool hand to his forehead. 'You've got a bit of a temperature,' she said.

'It's nothing. I'm OK. It's just hot in here.'

'You've had a lot to deal with lately, what with all your training and Dad coming home and then seeing Mark again.'

'Yeah,' said Ash. 'I suppose so.'

'You should take it easy now until the race. You need plenty of sleep and good food. Mum's orders. No more of these punishing training runs. You're supposed to wind down your training before a big race anyway, so a couple of days of rest won't hurt.'

He looked at her. Her angular, almost beautiful face. The delicate shadows under her eyes. She looked tired and sad.

'Mum,' he said. 'The other night. Dad went out, really late. I followed him.'

'He went out?' Worry creasing her forehead. 'What night was this?'

'The night before he took me out fishing and had a meltdown on Tolley Carn.'

'Why didn't you tell me this before?'

'I don't know. Because you were already so worried, I suppose.'

'You don't need to protect me, Ash. In fact, I'd rather you didn't try. I need to know what's going on, no matter what it is. Where did he go? What did he do?'

'He went to Stag's Leap first, then the Cullen farm. He just stood there, at the gate, staring at the house. Then he saw me. I think he knew I was there all along actually but he didn't let on. We walked home together. He seemed OK, just a bit down, that's all.'

Mum gave a small, sad smile. 'It's not so strange,' she said. 'Not if you think about it. Tom and him, they went back a long way. They were close friends when they were boys. Like you and Mark.'

'Yeah, that's what Dad said.'

'He misses Tom more than he lets on. Did he tell you that Tom once saved his life?'

'Yes. He said something happened on the Leap when he was the stag boy, and Tom pulled him back from the edge.'

'It won't always be like this, you know,' Mum said. 'Things will get better, I promise.'

'Yeah,' he said, turning away from her. 'But when, Mum?'

She stood up, went to the door. 'I still think you've got a touch of fever,' she said. 'Try to get some more sleep, then rest for today. No more running until the Stag Chase. Promise me?'

'OK,' he said. Closing his eyes, already drifting towards sleep again, Mum's voice mingling with half-formed dreams.

TWENTY~TWO

He heard the door click shut as Mum went out. Heat wrapped around him like a warm, wet blanket. Even with the curtains drawn, with his eyes closed, there was an aching brightness. He tossed and turned and couldn't get comfortable.

A tinny crackle of music from the radio downstairs. A dog barking in the distance.

A rook flying straight at the window, beak the colour of iron, claws hooked out.

He sat bolt upright.

No rook at the window now. Nothing but pale sky.

He got dressed, carefully rolling his T-shirt down over his bandaged chest. Then he went downstairs to the kitchen. The house was quiet and felt empty, though he knew Dad was almost certainly upstairs, shut in his darkened room as usual.

Sometimes it felt as if his dad was slowly ceasing to exist, his presence fading a little more every day.

Ash glanced at the wall clock. Two o'clock in the afternoon.

By now, Callie had probably found Mark, talked to him. Ash thought about going to Mark's camp again to look for them, but he knew instinctively that it was a bad idea. Callie had told him to keep away and she'd be furious if he barged in. When she was ready, she'd tell him all about it. He just had to trust her and wait.

He remembered the book they'd looked at in the library, the reference to a standing stone with a stag's head carved into it, and to somewhere called Corbie Tor. Landscape features he'd never heard of before, never knowingly seen.

He made himself a sandwich and went back up to his bedroom, eating as he searched online for Corbie Tor. It didn't take long to find it, in an article on an antiquarian maps website. An 'obsolete archaic place name', the article said. At least that explained why he'd never heard of it before. He clicked on a link and an image of an old map opened up. It was clumsily drawn, a crude sketch of the mountainous region northwest of Thornditch. But it was accurate enough for him to work out where Corbie Tor was.

He'd been there before, without knowing its name. The rocky outcrop he'd climbed when he'd found the wolf-dog, above the valley where Bone Jack lived.

He could go there again this afternoon, look around, see if he could find the standing stone. It probably wasn't important, probably didn't mean anything or have any sort of significance, but it was another piece of the jigsaw puzzle. And there was a chance he'd see Bone Jack again out there too. The thought made him edgy but he didn't care any more. The Stag Chase was the day after to-morrow and he wanted to find out whatever he could before he ran.

He pulled on his trainers. He'd promised Mum he wouldn't run today and he was still tired so he took his bike. The bike was faster anyway, a mean-looking hardtail he'd bought two summers ago after saving up for a whole year. He rode on the lanes and the main walking trails, then along the old drovers' paths. He stopped. This was where he'd found the wolf-dog, he was sure of it. Nothing there now, no sign that the wolf-dog had ever existed. But that didn't matter. He remembered the spot well enough. That dip in the path. That steep bank. Corbie Tor itself.

And in the valley below, the thorn trees and stony ground where Bone Jack's bothy was.

He left the bike at the side of the path and climbed up onto the higher ground above it.

Ahead stood a lone figure, silhouetted against the sky. Callie.

He frowned slightly, wondering what she was doing out here, where Mark was.

She started heading north and he followed. The air so still that every sound he made seemed huge. The crackle of the dry heather underfoot, the rasp of his breath.

Callie reached Corbie Tor and vanished around the other side of it.

Ash followed.

Now he heard voices. Callie's voice and then Mark's. Ash stopped and listened. He couldn't make out their words but he heard a gentleness in Mark's voice, a kindness that Ash had almost forgotten he was capable of.

He went closer, saw them walk out from the shadow of Corbie Tor and onto the lower path. Mark half naked, clay daubed, his hair sticking up in stiff spikes. He looked like some wild warrior from the ancient past, and Callie, with the mountain breeze tugging at her hair, seemed no less wild than her brother.

There was a closeness about them Ash had never really noticed before. He saw it now, in the way they moved with the same loose, easy strides, and the way word and gesture shifted between them, subtle and somehow secretive.

Suddenly he felt like an intruder. Callie had told him to stay away, to let her talk to Mark alone. He should go.

He turned to leave, started walking back towards where he'd left the bike. Then he stopped, annoyed with himself. He was part of this madness too, caught up in everything just like they were. He had every right to be there with them. There were things he needed to know, questions he just couldn't let go.

So he called out to them and Mark glanced back and the spell broke.

They waited for him to catch up, watched him blunder towards them through the bracken.

Callie glared at him. 'I told you not to come.'

'I wasn't looking for you or Mark,' said Ash. 'I thought you'd be at his camp in the woods, not out here.'

'So why did you come here?'

'I was looking for the places we read about in that book. I was curious. It's not important though. If you want me to go away, I'll go.'

She scowled at him. 'You might as well stay, now you're here.'

They walked on in silence, following Mark.

The sun bright in Ash's eyes. The salt taste of sweat on his cracked lips. Midges danced about him. He swatted them away and tried to catch Callie's attention again but she avoided looking at him. He understood. She was here for Mark, not for him.

They stopped.

Gorse, bracken, heather. A high thread of skylark song.

'What now?' said Ash.

Mark pointed towards a spike of rock Ash had never seen before, jutting from a bed of heather. It was maybe three metres tall, solitary, bleak. The standing stone mentioned in the book he and Callie had looked at in the library. It had to be.

'Is that what you came to find?' said Mark.

Ash nodded. 'The standing stone, yeah.'

They went up to it.

At first all Ash could see was pitted, weather-worn stone, scabbed with lichen. Then he ran his fingertips over the sun-warmed surface and from the rough contours a shape started to emerge.

Antlers. A stag's head. And not just a head. He could make out a torso and limbs as well. A figure that was half man, half stag. It felt wild and powerful.

Mark laughed. 'Do you know what it is?'

'Of course I know what it is,' said Ash. 'It's a stag boy.'

173

'Well done. Why do you think it's here, on this stone?'

'I don't know. It's ancient. Some sort of marker, maybe a religious thing. Something to do with the Stag Chase. I don't know.'

'It's where they used to sacrifice the stag boys, in the early days. They'd drag them here, cut their throats and their blood would run down the stone into the earth. Later on, when the holy men came and preached against human sacrifice, they stopped bringing the stag boys here. They chased them off the Leap instead, or threw them off. Far from the priests' prying eyes. That's where the Leap gets its name from. Stag's Leap, the stag boy's leap.'

'How do you know all that?'

'I just know,' said Mark.

Ash looked at Callie. She didn't look angry any more, just tired, defeated somehow, her face drawn and her eyes bright with tears.

'The old days are gone,' said Ash. 'No one is sacrificed these days. It's just a race now.'

'Most of the time it's just a race,' said Mark. 'Not this year though. You know. You've seen things. You know.'

'I don't know what I've seen, not really. All I know is that a few things have happened that I can't explain and there are a lot of old legends and ghost stories about dark stuff from the past.'

'Dark stuff from the past,' said Mark. 'That's right. That's why you've got to pull out of the Stag Chase. I'm serious, Ash. Pretend you've torn a muscle or something. They can find another stag boy. There's still time.'

'This again.' Ash blinked the sunlight from his eyes. 'What do you want, Mark? Why are you doing all this?'

'I told you. I want my dad back. I want everything to go back to the way it was.'

'What about Callie? What about what she wants?'

'I know what's best for my own sister.'

Callie lifted her head. Her face was pale, her grey eyes dark and fierce. She glared at Mark. 'This isn't best for me,' she said. 'All this – it's crazy. No one's going to be killed. Nothing's going to bring Dad back. He's gone. This is it, this is all we've got. The three of us, and Grandpa. And Grandpa's ill. We should be with him, we should be helping him. Not standing around out here in the middle of nowhere, talking about killing stag boys.'

'Callie—' Mark took a step towards her but she backed away.

'I can't listen to you any more,' she said. 'I can't listen to all this talk about Dad, about killing people. Stop it. You have to stop it.'

She retreated further away from them.

'Callie,' said Ash, 'it's OK. Please don't...'

But she wouldn't even look at him. Instead she turned, ran off up the path.

Ash started to follow her but Mark stopped him. 'Let her go. She doesn't get it.'

'Doesn't get what?' said Ash. 'That you think if you paint yourself with clay and kill rooks and murder the stag boy then that's going to bring your dad back? No one comes back from the dead. No one. Even if you really do kill me or some other stag boy, it won't bring your dad back.'

'You're wrong,' said Mark. His voice was quiet and deadly serious. 'You can bring people back. There's a way. Blood for blood, life for life.'

'What way?'

Mark glanced towards Bone Jack's bothy in the valley below. 'Him,' he said. 'Bone Jack. The guardian of the boundary between life and death. Get past him and you can get past death itself.'

'So what's the big plan?' said Ash. 'You're going to sacrifice the stag boy and Bone Jack's going to let you bring your father back from the dead? That's insane.'

Mark's eyes glittered. 'You don't even know who Bone Jack is, what he is.'

'He's just a man,' said Ash, even though he didn't

believe it. 'He's just a weird man, a hermit who lives in the mountains.'

'He's a shaman. He moves between the land of the living and the land of the dead. He's thousands of years old and he shapeshifts. He's a man, he's a bird, a thousand birds.'

'He's just a man,' said Ash again.

'He's much more than that,' said Mark. 'You know it as well as I do. He's much more than a man, but when he shapeshifts, when he breaks apart into rooks, then I can get at him. I kill his rooks, a few here, a few there. Every time I do it, he gets weaker. When I take the rooks and make them mine, I take his strength. And when I've taken enough of it, I'll be able to do what he can do. I'll go into Annwn, into the realm of the dead, and I'll bring back my dad.'

'So that's why you're really out here? Waiting for Bone Jack to shapeshift so you can kill some more rooks, take his power and travel to the land of the dead? Do you know how crazy that sounds?'

'I don't care how it sounds.'

'How do you kill the rooks anyway?'

'Catapult,' said Mark. 'Remember how we used to practise hitting empty tin cans? I was good at it. I'm even better now.'

'Mark,' said Ash, 'you're ill. You should come home with me. Please, come home with me.'

'I'm not ill,' said Mark. 'I'm not going anywhere. You know I'm not crazy. You know what I'm saying is true.'

Ash looked away from him, looked beyond the standing stone. There was something else out there, further along the path, a familiar shape silhouetted against the sky.

He went towards it.

The stag's head, the one Mark had worn as a headdress when he'd dressed up as the stag god. Stuck on a pole. Its eyes gone, eaten away. Its coat dull, matted with dried blood. Flies droning around it.

Ash turned away from it and walked back towards Mark. Mark smiled weirdly, eyes flint-hard. Ash watched him smirk and swagger, pleased with the shock on Ash's face.

'I'm going to run in the Stag Chase,' said Ash, suddenly cold with fury. 'I'm going to run for my dad. I'm going to run all your ghosts into the ground. You can't stop me.'

He kept walking, left Mark behind. He climbed up Corbie Tor. He looked down across the valley to where Bone Jack's bothy stood among the thorn trees.

On the ridge beyond, dark birds gathered like a storm

cloud. They flowed and eddied in the warm air, flapped apart, drew together again, closer now, denser, wings touching, melting into each other until the flock became a shadow, an outline. The silhouette of a man in a long coat, a wide-brimmed hat.

Ash glanced down to where Mark had been standing but Mark was nowhere to be seen. Run off to find Callie, Ash thought.

He was alone except for Bone Jack, the wild man, the shapeshifter, dark against the skyline. Ash watched him stride away until he couldn't see him any more.

Then, without knowing quite why he did it, he ran downhill towards Bone Jack's bothy.

TWENTY~THREE

Ash stood outside the bothy. He didn't have a plan, didn't know what to do, what he was looking for. Something, anything, that might give him an edge.

The bone strings in the doorway rattled in the breeze. Beyond them was deep shadow. Just like last time, except now the filthy windows were blank and there was no blurry face staring through at him.

He listened. All he heard was the slow slide of his own breathing, the whisper of the breeze among the thorn trees, bird chatter.

No sign of Bone Jack.

He pushed through the bone strings into hot dusty gloom. Sweat prickled on his skin. He stopped just inside, waited for his eyes to adjust to the dark. Taut threads of sunlight cut through the grime on the windows. The tiny skulls on the bone strings threw weird shadows against the back wall.

Now he could make out shapes in the gloom. A small table with two chairs. A woodstove with a stack of firewood next to it. A pile of blankets and furs at one end of the room.

It seemed more like a den than a home.

Something moved, fluttered and flapped. A tiny bird, a wren or something. It shot past him, out through the bone curtain.

He went further inside. A fox skull on a shelf, an old army knife, five stones set out side by side on the table. He picked one up, felt its weight and balance. Leaf-shaped, shiny, cool against his skin. A flint arrowhead.

Next to the arrowheads was a book. It was small, bound with old soft leather. He opened it. The thin pages were so fragile that he imagined even the gentlest touch of his fingertips might tear them. Something written on them, a poem, handwritten in inky lettering.

'You again, lad,' said a voice behind him.

Ash spun round, still clutching the book. Fear shook through him.

Bone Jack in the doorway, silhouetted against the bright sunlight outside. 'What is it this time? Another sick wolf? Thieving? Snooping?'

Ash shot a panicky glance across at the nearest window, briefly wondered if it would break if he hurled himself against it.

'I saw you over yon with the girl and the painted boy,' said Bone Jack. 'The crazy boy who's been killing my rooks.'

'He's killing them to take your power. You could stop him. You should stop him.'

'I can't stop him. Things has to play out as they will for the living. It's not for me to interfere.'

His eyes sharp and cold and pale as ice.

'Are you human?' said Ash. The words rushing out, taking him by surprise. 'Or something else? A spirit or a myth thing, like Taliesin or the Green Man?'

'They're just names,' said Bone Jack. 'Names and stories.'

'OK,' said Ash. Fear twisted inside him. Suddenly he wanted to get out of the bothy but Bone Jack was between him and the doorway. He took a deep breath to steady his nerves. 'I came here to find some answers, that's all. There are ghosts in the mountains. I've seen them. There was that wolf. And Mark's saying he's going to kill the stag boy and bring his dad back from the dead and somehow it all seems to have something to do with you.'

As he spoke, he took a step towards the door. Legs heavy as wood, sweating so much his shirt was sticking to his back.

Bone Jack stayed where he was, blocking the only way out.

'It ain't about me,' said Bone Jack. 'It's about the dying land and the old ways.'

'That's what Mark said. The old ways. Life for life. The stag boy's life in exchange for his dad's.'

'The dead stay dead,' said Bone Jack. 'Only ghosts come back.'

'Like those hound boys?'

'Aye.'

'Why have they come back?'

'They're here every year, every Stag Chase. Most years there's nowt much to them. But now the land's sick and its darkest dreams are rising from it like mist. The sicker the land is, the stronger they get.'

'What do they want?'

'Blood and death is what. It's all they know. How to hunt, how to kill.'

'Why don't you stop them?'

'They ain't strong enough yet.'

'I don't know what that means.'

No response. Bone Jack's face was hidden in the

shadow under the brim of his hat and suddenly Ash couldn't catch his breath. The gloom pressed in around him, thick with ancient dust, and all he could think about was getting outside, into fresh air and sunlight and limitless space.

'I'll go now,' he said. His voice was a croak. He took a small step towards the door, then another. 'I'm sorry I disturbed you.'

He kept his gaze low, kept moving, slow tiny paces.

And Bone Jack stepped aside to let him out.

Ash kept walking until he was halfway across the clearing. Then he stopped, his fear fading in the sunlight. He looked back at Bone Jack.

'I don't know what to do,' said Ash. 'What should I do?'

'Hold to your own, lad.'

'What does that mean?'

But Bone Jack had already turned away, retreated into the gloom behind the bone strings.

Ash ran on through the trees and up the slope back towards Corbie Tor. Halfway, he stopped.

He was still holding the book he'd picked up in the bothy.

He sat on a slab of rock and stared at it. There was a faint trace of lettering on the cover, so faded that he could barely make out the words. He angled the book into the sunlight, squinted at it, spoke its title out loud: *The Battle of the Trees*.

He'd come across that title before. Where? He trawled his memory. Then it came back to him. He'd seen it when he'd looked up Bone Jack online and learned about his connection to those other mysterious wild men of the mountains. Taliesin, he thought. *The Battle of the Trees* was a poem written by Taliesin.

The breeze gusted, hot and dry.

He opened the book and started to read.

> *I have been in a multitude of shapes,*
> *Before I assumed a consistent form.*
> *I have been a sword, narrow, variegated,*
> *I will believe when it is apparent.*
> *I have been a tear in the air,*
> *I have been the dullest of stars.*
> *I have been a word among letters,*
> *I have been a book in the origin.*
> *I have been the light of lanterns,*
> *A year and a half.*

A poem about shapeshifting.

The breeze blew harder, lashed tears from his eyes and

tore at the tissue-thin pages. Ash slammed the book shut and shielded it from the wind with his body. But it broke into pieces in his hands. Shreds of paper danced like flakes of ash across the mountainside. Nothing left in his hands except a few limp scraps of old leather.

Gone. Just the echo of the poem in his mind.

I have been in a multitude of shapes...

Birdman. Shapeshifter.

Bone Jack.

The wind dropped. He stood up.

In his mind, he heard Bone Jack's voice again. *Hold to your own, lad.*

'What did you mean?' Ash said, out loud.

Perhaps Bone Jack had meant that he should make his own choices and stand by them. Or that he should take care of his own – of Mum and Dad – and leave the rest alone. But maybe Mark and Callie were his own too.

Every answer only seemed to lead to more questions. And maybe none of it mattered anyway. Maybe the only thing that mattered was the one thing he could do: run.

Only tomorrow to get through and then it would be Sunday, the day of the Stag Chase. Until then, he'd sleep, chill out, play computer games, load up on carbs, keep his head down. Then on Sunday he'd run. Everything was simple when he ran, just muscle and bone, rhythm and focus and the lie of the land. Nothing and no one would catch him. He'd outrun them all. Mark, the hound boys, the ghosts. He'd leave them all trailing in his wake. He'd run his race his own way, and Dad would be waiting for him at the finish line. It would be all right. He just had to run and everything would be all right.

A movement below in the valley caught his eye. Rooks, flapping up from the thorn trees.

The air thrummed with their wing beats. They scattered across the land, night-black rags tossed on the wind, and he watched them until they were gone.

TWENTY~FOUR

That night, Ash slept deeply, dreamlessly. When he woke, the house was quiet. These days, it was nearly always quiet. Almost two weeks since Dad came home, and the silence and tension almost seemed ordinary now. Mum either in the garden or out somewhere. Dad curled up in the dark in his room. A new normal they'd all somehow fallen into, learned to live with.

He glanced at his alarm clock. Just gone eight thirty. Saturday morning.

The Stag Chase tomorrow.

Excitement and fear burned through him. He rolled out of bed, got dressed, went downstairs. He stopped on the landing and knocked softly on the door to Dad's room. No response, but he switched on the light and went in anyway.

The bed was empty and unmade. Sheets trailing to the

floor. The rucksack slumped against the wall, still spilling clothes. The air sour with sweat and dread.

Dad was next to the window, squatting on his heels with his back to the wall. He was twitchy. He kept sniffing as if he had a cold. Rubbed his hand over his face again and again. In the hard white light, he looked grey and ill.

'What's wrong, Dad? What are you doing down there? Dad? Are you OK?'

No reply.

Ash picked his way through all the junk to where Dad was. He pulled back the curtains and opened the window. Fresh air, sunlight, and a rush of birdsong.

'Shut the window!' hissed Dad. 'Shut the curtains.'

Ash stared at him. 'Come on, Dad. Get up. Please get up, Dad.'

'Shut the window,' said Dad again. 'Shut the curtains.'

Silently Ash did as he said. He switched off the light, closed the door behind him. He trembled and felt sick. As if the world had tilted and everything had rearranged itself in ways he couldn't understand. Something gone wrong, gone askew, throwing everything out of kilter. He had to put it right but he didn't even know what it was, never mind how to fix it.

He went outside. He sat on the doorstep and stared at the sun until it burned away everything, land and sky and memory.

A car came along the lane, pulled up. A door slamming.

Footfalls crunching on the gravel drive.

Ash turned his head, blinking, his eyes still full of fierce sunlight.

A silhouette against the sun glare. Featureless, a shadow. Ash squinted at it.

The figure came closer, shimmering like a dark mirage. 'I'm looking for your mother,' it said. A woman's voice. Ash stood up, lost his balance, caught himself.

'Is your mother home?'

'No. I don't think so.'

'Well, don't you know?'

Now the dazzle faded from his eyes and he could make out a bulky outline, a fluffy halo of honey-coloured hair. Then he knew who she was and panic flared inside him.

'You're her,' he said. 'Grandpa Cullen's next-door neighbour.'

'Mrs Hopkinson,' she said. 'And I need to talk to your mother.'

It had to be about Mark and Callie. And it was Ash's fault. He'd told her his name and she'd known who he was and where he lived, even though he'd lied to her. She'd realised that it meant Mark and Callie couldn't be living with relatives in Thornditch after all.

Now here she was. And he had to get rid of her.

'Mum's not in.'

'We'll see, shall we?'

She went to the door, rang the bell.

They waited.

'I told you,' said Ash. 'She's not home.'

Then the door opened. Mum in her floppy hat, secateurs in her hand, looking from Mrs Hopkinson to Ash and back again.

'I need to talk to you,' Mrs Hopkinson said. 'About Mark and Callie Cullen. In private.'

Ash caught Mum's eye, willed her to understand, not to say something that would have search parties scouring the mountains. Mum frowned slightly, then waved Mrs Hopkinson inside and closed the door.

It was half an hour before Mrs Hopkinson left. Ash watched her go, listened to her car drive away. Then he went to find Mum.

'What did she want?'

'You know what she wanted. She's worried about Mark and Callie. Apparently Mark told her that they were staying with relatives here in Thornditch, then you

SARA CROWE

turned up in Coldbrook looking for them and she worked out they couldn't possibly be in Thornditch after all.'

'So what did you tell her?'

'I told her that Mark must have thought they were coming to Thornditch but that they'd gone to stay with some other relatives instead, further away.'

'You lied to her?'

'I'm not proud of it,' said Mum. 'She's just concerned, that's all. She came all the way out here because she's worried about them. She's a nice woman. I don't like lying to her. I don't like lying to anyone.'

'So why did you?'

'Because those kids have been through far too much already. If she reports them as missing, social services will get involved and they'll come looking for Callie.'

'What about Mark?'

'Mark is sixteen, a few months older than you. Legally he's old enough to leave home. But Callie is only fourteen. They'd come for her and take her away. That child has suffered more than her share of loss and upheaval lately.'

'Thanks, Mum.'

'Don't thank me,' she said. 'This is a serious matter. I lied to Mrs Hopkinson and Callie is out there somewhere fending for herself. I don't like lying, and if anything happens to Callie, it will be my fault. So next time you see her, I want you to get her to come and talk to me so we can sort something out for her. OK?'

'OK.' He hesitated. 'Mum?'

'What now?'

'I went into Dad's room earlier. He's crouching in there, in the dark, by the window.'

'I know,' she said. 'He's been like that for a few hours. He's having a bad day.'

'He's not going to make it to the Stag Chase tomorrow, is he?'

'We'll see. He might have a better day tomorrow.' Her face softened and she smiled. 'What about you? Are you ready for the race?'

'Yeah, as ready as I'll ever be.'

'You'll be fine. I know you will.'

He looked at her and felt a million miles from her. She knew nothing about Mark's threats or spectral hound boys with murder in their eyes or Bone Jack. To her, the Stag Chase was just a race and all he had to worry about was running. And that was how it had to be. If he'd told her even half of it, she'd think he'd gone as crazy as Dad and then she'd have nothing, no one to turn to.

So he smiled and said, 'Yeah, I'll be fine.'

'Any plans for today?' she said.

He laughed. 'Big plans to play computer games, eat a lot of carbs, lounge around and sleep as much as I can.'

'You'd better get on with it then,' said Mum.

Ash was sure he'd lie awake half the night, fretting about the race, about Dad, about Mark. Instead he fell into a deep, black, dreamless sleep almost immediately his head hit the pillow.

Then something woke him. He lay in the moon-washed dark, his eyes wide open, his heart racing.

It came again, a thud, then a grunt of breath.

He got out of bed, opened the curtain and looked out.

He expected to see hound boys gathered outside again. But this time there was only one boy out there in the moonlight, bone-white under a ragged black cloak and with the monstrous stag's head upon his shoulders.

Ash knew it was Mark, in his stag-god guise, but still his heart quickened and a chill ran through him. A thin pain threaded along the cuts on his chest, as if the ghost of the knife was retracing its bloody path across his skin.

Mark didn't look up. He raised one foot and brought it down hard, then the other foot, again and again, slowly at first, building to a steady rhythm. He raised his arms and the cloak hung from them like half-opened wings. Then he danced, circling like a huge grotesque bird. He didn't look up. Whatever this was, it wasn't meant for Ash's eyes.

So what was it? Maybe a pre-Stag Chase ritual. Maybe something else.

Ash pulled on a T-shirt and went downstairs.

By the time he got outside, Mark was gone.

He'd left the stag's head behind, propped upright in the middle of the moon-silvered lawn. It seemed to watch Ash from the inky hollows where its eyes had once been. Bone gleamed through its tattered hide. The stench of death hung in the still night air, corrupt and sickly sweet.

He couldn't leave it here for Mum to find in the morning. She'd freak. But he couldn't shove it under the hedge like he'd done with the sheep skull. The antlers were too big, too unwieldy, and the hedge wouldn't hide the stink of it anyway.

Breathing through his mouth to avoid the smell, he grasped the antlers and lifted. It was heavy, strapped to a clumsy wooden structure that Mark must have added so he could position it on his shoulders, the stag's head raised above his own. Ash held it at arm's length and tried not to think about the putrefying flesh and the likelihood of maggots, or about Mark, so far gone in his madness that he could bear to wear the foul thing.

He carried it into the lane, then swung it up over the hedge into the field opposite the house. It crunched down somewhere in the darkness beyond, among nettles and foxgloves.

He went back to the house, headed straight for the kitchen. He took a clean cloth from the cupboard under the sink, ran it under the hot tap and squirted hand-wash gel all over it. He washed his hands, his arms, his legs, everywhere the stag's rotten head might have touched him or dripped putrid filth on him.

A door opened upstairs, the pad of footsteps on the landing then coming down the stairs. Mum. She must have heard him moving around.

Quickly he dried himself with a tea towel then opened the fridge and pretended to root around inside it.

The kitchen door opened and he blinked owlishly at Mum.

'It's two o'clock in the morning,' she said. 'What are you doing in here?'

'I couldn't sleep,' Ash said.

'So you thought you'd come downstairs and make yourself a snack, I suppose?'

He grinned sheepishly. 'I was hungry.'

'You shouldn't eat this late at night, especially when you've got a race to run in a few hours' time. Come on, back up to bed with you.'

He shut the fridge door, followed Mum upstairs. 'Try to get some sleep,' she said. 'And if you can't sleep, at least get some rest.'

Back in his bedroom, he glanced out of the window again. The night was still, silent except for the fluting call of a tawny owl. It was as if Mark had never been there.

Ash lay down on the bed and closed his eyes. He was too tired now to worry any more about Mark or anything much. He felt weirdly calm, detached from everything. He knew the feeling wouldn't last but for now he let himself drift with it. Morning would come. The Stag Chase would go ahead. And what would be, would be.

TWENTY~FIVE

He slept until seven, woke to a jabber of voices on his radio alarm. For a few minutes he didn't move, just lay with his eyes wide open, staring at the patterns of hazy sunlight playing across the ceiling. This was it. The day of the Stag Chase. Today anything could happen, glory or disgrace, life or death.

Glory. Let it be glory.

He got out of bed, pulled on his tracksuit and running shoes, went downstairs.

Mum was in the kitchen.

'Morning,' he said. 'Where's Dad?'

'He's not up yet, love,' said Mum.

'But he knows, right? He knows it's the Stag Chase today?'

'Yes, he knows. He'll come down soon, I'm sure.' But she didn't sound sure. 'Sit down and I'll get you some breakfast,' she said. 'Come on. Stop worrying about Dad.'

'Right,' said Ash. He sat at the table. Mum put a bowl of porridge in front of him. Now he felt sick, nerves jumping like grasshoppers in his stomach. He forced himself to eat, gluey spoonful after gluey spoonful. Then a slice of toast spread with peanut butter and honey.

Quarter to eight and still no sign of Dad. Ash couldn't settle. 'I'll go wake him up,' he said.

The dark room again. The clogged air. Dad hunched on his side in the bed. Even before he spoke, Ash knew Dad wasn't going to make it. Today was another of his bad days.

'Dad,' he said, 'it's the Stag Chase today. You'll be there, won't you?'

Dad grunted.

'You promised, Dad.'

'Let me sleep,' said Dad.

'It's all you do,' said Ash. 'Sleep and mess things up.'

He shut the door hard behind him. Went downstairs, outside. He sat on the garden bench next to the wall, gazed with unfocused eyes above the trees to Tolley Carn, already smudged with heat.

Mum came out and sat down next to him. 'I thought we could go for a drive. Then I'll drop you off in the village in time for the race.'

Ash shook his head. 'I don't want to go.'

'For a drive or to the race?'

'Both.'

'You'll regret it if you don't run. Probably for the rest of your life.'

'I don't care.'

'Yes, you do. You've spent months training for this. And I know Dad hasn't got his act together yet today, but he's so proud of you. He'll be there when you race. I know he will.'

'How do you know?'

'Because I know how much he loves you.'

Ash sighed. He was acting like a brat again. And she was right. She was nearly always right. 'OK,' he said. 'You win.'

'I win an hour in a car with a sulky teenager,' she said. 'Great.'

He smiled in spite of himself.

They went out along the mountain roads. Mum didn't talk and Ash watched through the window as the land scrolled past like film scenery, mountains and valleys carved by vast forces of ice, water, wind, sculpted over billions of years. So ancient it seemed it must always have been there, must always have looked like this. But Ash knew it owed its very form to change, to the slow forces of the elements that shaped it. Nothing stayed the same for ever, not really. Not people, not families, not even the land itself. All you could do was hold on as best you could.

They stopped on the road halfway up Owl Cry Ridge, got out of the car, sat on a patch of scratchy brown grass. The breeze was cool against Ash's skin.

'Feeling any better now?' said Mum.

Ash nodded. 'Yeah. A bit.'

'He'll be OK, you know. Your dad. It'll take time and there'll be ups and downs, but he'll get there.'

'Do you really believe that?'

She smiled and shrugged. 'Most of the time.'

Ash watched a distant kestrel pause in the sky then drop like a stone into the heather. 'Why?' he said. 'Why him? I don't get it. Other soldiers come home and they're OK.'

'Some soldiers come home in body bags,' said Mum. 'Some come home with arms or legs missing, or in wheelchairs. Your dad came home with post-traumatic stress disorder. There's no why about it. Some soldiers get it and others don't.'

'He's scared,' said Ash. 'He's jumping at shadows all the time. He's scared of everything.'

SARA CROWE

'Your dad is one of the bravest men I know,' said Mum.

'Maybe he used to be,' said Ash. 'But he's changed. He's like a completely different person. I don't get it.'

Mum was quiet, gazing across the valley into the distance, something frozen and faraway in her expression.

'Is he always going to be like this?' he said.

'No, not always. People with post-traumatic stress, well, it can come and go. And if they get help, counselling, maybe medication for a while if they need it . . . it's manageable. They can recover, lead normal lives.'

'I keep getting angry with him,' said Ash. 'I know he can't help it, I know he's ill, but I still keep thinking that if he wanted to, if he really loved us, he'd get better. He'd get help. He'd go and see that counsellor. He'd try. But he isn't trying. He just shuts himself up in his room and I don't know what to do.'

'You don't need to do anything,' said Mum. 'Just run your race and then we'll take things one day at a time.'

She got to her feet. 'Come on. It's time we headed back to Thornditch.'

Ash nodded, stood up.

'Anything else you'd like to do before the race starts?'

Ash thought for a moment. 'Yeah,' he said. 'I want to go to the churchyard.'

Mum raised her eyebrows. 'The churchyard? What for?'

'I don't know,' said Ash. 'I suppose because Tom Cullen saved Dad's life when Dad was the stag boy. It just feels like something I should do, before the race. Pay my respects.'

But it was more than that. Tom Cullen's death was the reason Mark was running with ghosts and making crazy threats to kill the stag boy. He was at the heart of everything Mark had done, everything Mark would do, and yet he was dead and gone, an absence around which chaos swirled. Ash wanted to stand at his grave. He wanted Tom Cullen to be just Mark and Callie's dad again, just Dad's best friend again. A real person who had lived and died.

The main street was closed when they got there. Traffic cones and detour signs stood at either end to keep out cars. A crowd was already gathering, a mix of locals and tourists. People were setting up food stalls and souvenir stalls decked out with T-shirts, baseball caps, mugs and key rings, all bearing the stag's head emblem. The new local economy, selling tat to tourists looking for a bit of Merrie Olde England.

They left the car in a lay-by and walked towards the churchyard. Through the gate under the wooden arch, along the stone path that wound among the graves. Ash stopped at Tom Cullen's grave, a shiny rectangle of polished granite with gold lettering cut and painted into it. *Beloved father to Mark and Callie.* There were still flowers on the grave, withered and dry, their colours faded.

'I was scared of him,' said Ash. 'He never smiled. He hardly ever spoke except to tell us what to do.'

'He wasn't always like that,' said Mum. 'He used to be great fun. A bit wild until he married Ella and they had the kids. He loved being a dad. He took those kids all over the mountains, taught them about wildlife and nature. He knew the name of every plant and every bird and bug, did Tom. Your dad used to say he knew the name of every pebble, too. Then Ella got sick and died.'

Ash had a brief flash of a dark-haired woman with laughter in her eyes. 'I don't remember her very well,' he said. 'Just what she looked like.'

'Mark was only eight when she died so you must have been seven. It seems such a long time ago. Tom was heartbroken and all alone out here with two young kids to look after and a farm to run. He kind of withdrew into himself. He wouldn't accept any help, but he should have. He needed it. The kids needed it. I guess by the time the foot-and-mouth hit, he was already at breaking point. He didn't have anything left for another crisis.'

'Dad told me he feels guilty for not being there to help him.'

'Dad was thousands of miles away,' said Mum. 'Risking his life and serving his country.'

Ash nodded. He gazed down at the dead flowers. There was something tucked in among them, catching the sunlight. He crouched and picked it up. Card inside a clear plastic sleeve. He turned it over.

It was a small photograph, one he'd never seen before. He recognised the setting straightaway though: the upper slope of Stag's Leap. It was a sunny day and Tom Cullen was standing with a dark-haired little girl on his shoulders, her hands clamped over his eyes. They were both laughing. Next to him, smiling broadly, stood Ash's own dad and in front of them were two boys, four or five years old. Mark, sturdy and brown, smiling at something or someone outside the frame. And Ash, slighter and more serious, watching Mark.

'What's that?' said Mum.

He showed her the photograph. 'Were you there as well?'

'I expect so,' she said. 'When your dad was home on leave, we sometimes used to take picnics up there with you kids. Ella, Mark's mum, was always taking pictures. This must be one of hers.'

Ash tucked the photograph back among the dead flowers.

They walked slowly back to the road.

'You go and do whatever it is you have to do before the race starts,' said Mum. 'I'll go home. See what's going on. I'll make sure your dad gets here. I promise.'

Ash nodded. He watched her walk back to the car, wave, drive away.

Then he drew a long breath and headed for the Huntsman Inn.

TWENTY~SIX

There was a TV crew in front of the inn. The camera trained on a shiny-faced reporter sweating in suit and tie, adjusting his smile. 'Today I'm in Thornditch for the historic Stag Chase,' he said. Then said it again and again, as if he was stuck on loop.

Ash slipped past the TV crew into the car park next to the inn. Bunting strung between the trees. Starlings squabbling in the high boughs. The air was already glassy with heat. Outside the inn, Morris dancers leaped and turned and clacked sticks like swords. Bells jangled below their knees. A man dressed in a shaggy costume of foliage skipped chaotically around them, then stopped and lifted his arms like boughs. He stared in Ash's direction, eyes bright and curious in a leafy mask.

At the edges of the crowd, the hound boys prowled. They were already kitted out in their long black shorts, vests, masks of paint-stiffened cloth. They struck poses for photographers. Howled and strutted for attention.

Rupert Sloper, the Master of Hounds, came round the side of the pub. Quick, anxious movements. His belt high and tight around his pot belly. His round pink face shone with sweat. He scanned the crowd, the hound boys, until he spotted Ash. He waved and hurried over. 'There you are!' he said. 'You're late. I was starting to think you weren't coming.'

'Sorry,' said Ash.

Sloper stared at him, annoyed.

'Family stuff,' said Ash. 'I couldn't get away.'

Sloper's expression softened. 'Ah. Your father, I suppose. I heard he was home and not quite himself...' He stopped, cleared his throat. 'I trust everything is all right now.'

Ash shrugged. 'I'm here, aren't I?'

'Yes, yes, you are,' said Sloper. 'Good. Well, this way then.'

He led Ash through a side door, along a gloomy corridor, into a small windowless room that smelled of stale beer. A bare light bulb gave out a harsh white glare. A table and a couple of chairs stood in one corner. A blotched mirror on the wall.

'Your kit's on the table. I'll wait outside the door while

you get changed, then I'll need to brief you about your destination.'

The secret destination, known to the Master of Hounds and soon to Ash as well but not to the hound boys.

Ash pulled on black knee-length shorts and a dull reddish-brown vest top. Then the half-mask, made of stiffened cloth, pale brown smudged with black in rough approximation of a stag's face. No antlers. He'd get to wear the antler headdress only if he won the race.

Last was a small backpack. Inside it were two bottles of water, a few energy bars, a tiny compass, plasters, a whistle for emergencies, an Ordnance Survey map.

His reflection gazed back at him from the mirror. In the mask, he seemed only partly himself. The other part was already the stag: wild, fearful, exhilarated.

He went back out into the corridor where Sloper was pacing and waiting.

'All set?' said Sloper.

Ash nodded. He watched Sloper through the eyeholes in the mask.

'Right then,' said Sloper. 'We're nearly done. Ready for your briefing?'

'Yeah.'

'Your destination is Black Crag. If you don't know

where it is, check the map in your pack. It's marked on there.'

'I know where it is.'

'Right. Good. At the summit of Black Crag, there's a cairn. It's a stack of stones, sort of cone-shaped, not quite as tall as you. Lift the top stone and underneath you'll find a pendant with a leather thong threaded through it. Put it around your neck and then get back here without getting caught by the hounds. That clear?'

'Yes,' said Ash. 'Head for Black Crag, retrieve the pendant from the cairn, get back here without getting caught.'

'Simple enough,' said Sloper. 'Good.'

Then came the safety briefing.

Drink plenty of water. There'll be extra on Black Crag, for if you need it.

Stay within the circle marked in red on the map.

In the event of injury or getting lost, stay where you are and wait for rescue. Blow the whistle once every two minutes to help the rescue team locate you.

If you're not back by 4 p.m., rescue teams will be sent out automatically to search for you.

'Don't take risks,' said Sloper. 'We don't want any broken bones or dead bodies.'

'I'll be careful.'

'Good lad. The horn will sound at ten sharp.' Sloper checked his watch. 'That's in another ten minutes. You'll set off first. Then you've got thirty minutes to get as far away as you can before the horn sounds again and the hounds set off after you.'

Ash nodded.

'Ready then?' said Sloper.

'Ready.'

He followed Sloper out into the bright sunlight. The hound boys circled and bayed, a wild excited ululation. They kept their distance, followed Ash with their eyes as they paced, already moving like predators.

Ash's stomach tightened.

They're just boys, he told himself. Boys in stupid masks. But they were more than that, he knew. Not just boys any more but actors in an ancient drama played out year after year for centuries. They were hounds and he was a stag and they would do everything in their power to hunt him down.

And he would do everything in his power to stay ahead of them.

He scanned the crowd again for Mum and Dad. No sign of them anywhere.

Disappointment hollowed his chest. All this work and effort, all those months of training, and Dad had just hidden away like a loser. There was no point in running the race if Dad wasn't there to see it, there to meet him at the finish. He might as well rip off the mask, walk away, go home, go out into the mountains, go anywhere but here.

The hound boys yowled and paced and panted.

Beyond them, onlookers pointed cameras at him.

One of the hound boys came closer. He skirted Ash like a wolf. Head down. Long slow strides. He looked different to the others. His mask was bone-white and blood-red. Arms, shoulders, legs streaked with charcoal and clay.

He stopped, stood with hands on hips and stared at Ash. Then he laughed.

Ash knew that laugh.

'Mark,' he said.

Above the clamour of the hounds he heard Sloper's voice over the tannoy, calling everyone to their places for the start of the race.

'You came then,' said Mark. 'You're going to be the stag boy, even though I warned you not to. I gave you a chance. Whatever happens now, it's on your head.'

'You're not going to kill me,' said Ash. 'You're not even going to catch me.'

Mark came closer, leaned into him. His breath hot

against Ash's ear. 'We're going to tear you apart, Ash Tyler,' he said. Then that singsong, whispery chant: 'Earth and stone, fire and ash, blood and bone.'

Ash shoved him, as hard as he could. Mark staggered back theatrically, then straightened. He stood there, laughed again. Then he turned away and went back among the circling hound boys, matching his pace and voice to theirs.

A musical blast ripped through the air, tailed off into a trembling wail. The hunting horn.

The crowd fell silent. All eyes on Ash.

And no sign of Dad.

Tears hot in his eyes. Everything – all his training, his dream of victory and Dad waiting proudly at the finish – would be for nothing if Dad wasn't there. He might as well just walk away. They'd watch and mutter and wonder about his reasons, his lack of character. Sloper would trot after him, all in a fluster, pleading with him. They'd blame him for ruining the day. But they couldn't stop him.

Run away from the race, from home, from Mark, all of it.

What then, Ash Tyler?

They'd get another boy to run, one of the hounds. Then maybe Mark really would go through with his plans, kill the stag boy in the belief that he could bring back his dad from Annwn, the Otherworld. He could tell Sloper, warn him about Mark's threats. But no one would believe him. They'd think everything was just the usual pre-Chase pranks, and Mark would laugh and agree with them and the Stag Chase would go ahead with or without him.

Besides, this was his responsibility. He was the stag boy. He was going to run this race for Dad, even if Dad wasn't there to see him do it.

He drew a slow, deep breath. Squared his shoulders and crossed to the starting line. Stretched, hopped from foot to foot, shook the tension from his body.

Sloper touched his arm. 'You remember what I told you and take care out there, lad. Remember it's just a race. Three more blasts on the horn now and you're away.'

Ash nodded.

The first blast sounded. The second.

The third.

TWENTY~SEVEN

Ash ran.

His legs felt like jelly. His chest was so tight he couldn't catch his breath. The faces in the crowd blurred. The cheering, whooping and clapping zoned into white noise.

He ran out of the car park, along the high street, past morris men and jugglers, hot-dog stalls and an ice-cream van and a stall selling stupid fake antlers attached to Alice bands.

The crowd thinned to nothing. Its clamour sank away behind him. He pushed the mask back over his head so he could see properly. He heard the steady thump of his heart, the wild song of his blood, his own sharp, shallow breaths. Beyond these, there was stillness, silence, space, and now he settled into his running, strong and steady.

He ran under the wooden arch that led into the churchyard, past Tom Cullen's grave, past the gnarly yew tree and a bramble-grown corner. Then he ducked through a leafy tunnel in the tall beech hedge and came out into bright sunlight. The sun at his back. He chased the long shadow of himself along the footpath through the fields to Tolley Carn, ran around it, skirted the tarn, headed into the folds of mountain and valley beyond. Here was where he'd throw the hounds off his trail, lose them among the creases and dips and humps of the lower slopes, hide in the gullies and behind rock stacks and crags. He'd keep to the little tracks, half hidden by gorse and bracken, stay below the skyline.

He was fast. He was silent. He was stealthy as a fox.

He headed west, along one of the faint and ancient footpaths spun like cobweb over the land. He slithered down a slick of tired grass to a dry streambed. Ran between ranks of tall reeds with seedheads like loose cotton-wool balls. The air like warm soup.

In the distance behind him, the thin rising wail of the hunting horn. The hound boys would be setting off now, running flat-out to catch up with him before he got too deep into the wild land.

Instinctively he picked up his pace.

He followed the streambed until it stopped at a wall of rock. Usually there was a waterfall here, a narrow torrent of clear cold mountain water that plunged into a seething pool. Now there was only a slick, slimy height with a stagnant greenish pool at its foot. Water boatmen skating on its surface. Midges storming above it.

He scrambled up the bank to the side of it, gorse ripping at his skin.

Ahead, Black Crag loomed against the skyline.

He paused in a shady hollow to catch his breath. Somewhere far behind him the hound boys would be fanning out, searching, trying to work out his route and his destination.

He left the streambed. He crossed a desert of sharp black shingle spiked with dead brown weeds. Sweat crawled down his face.

Black Crag, as raw as a mountain on the moon. Slopes of black scree, rock, burnt wiry grass. A faint path slashed its way to the summit in full view of anyone looking up from the valleys and ridges below. Everything else was climb or slither. There was no choice but to take the path.

Speed then, if he couldn't hide. It was too steep and unstable to run here, but he climbed fast. His breath sawing in and out. Sweat glittering on his skin. A knot of pain tightening in his right calf. He'd stretch it out when he found a hidden spot to grab a few moments of rest.

Up here, the wind was stronger and colder, respite from the heavy summer heat. By the time he was halfway up, the sun was no more than a white blur behind thickening grey cloud.

He passed a gorse bush sculpted by the wind into a sideways teardrop. Yellow flowers bright as flames. The path led between two tall stones leaning drunkenly towards each other. Beyond those, a torrent of scree lay between him and the peak. He started across it. Rock fragments skittered behind him and clacked their way down the mountain. He clambered over rock now, thick weatherworn slabs untidily piled up on each other. Ahead lay a craggy climb to the stacked stones of the cairn.

Below, mountain and valley stretched away into deepening murk. It wasn't eleven o'clock in the morning yet, but already it was as gloomy as dusk.

Summer coming to an end, today of all days.

He stopped to catch his breath and ease out the knot in his calf. On the mountainside across the valley, three figures picked their way up a steep path. Hound boys. He froze. He was out in the open, against the skyline. He cursed softly. They'd see him straight away if they glanced in his direction. Slowly he lowered himself into a crouch then inched behind the nearest jag of rock.

He peered around it. The hound boys were still trudging along the path, tiny figures moving in single file.

He watched them until they vanished around the side of the mountain.

They hadn't seen him. He was safe, for now. But he had to be more careful, keep a lookout, stay down low where there was less chance of being spotted.

He eyed the climb to the summit. It was raw, shelterless. Nowhere to hide if there were more hound boys moving through the nearby mountains.

He'd just have to risk it.

No path here, just a steep ascent over fissured jags of rock, sharp and gritty against his skin. He hauled himself up it by his fingertips and toes.

He pulled himself over the top, lay panting on a patch of hard dirt in the shade of the cairn.

He stood up, still breathing hard, and hefted away the cairn's top stone. It was heavier than he expected, a smooth weight that slipped through his fingers and clacked noisily down the slope. He froze. If the hound boys he'd seen earlier were still somewhere nearby, they'd surely have heard it. He looked around, listened. Silence. No sign of any movement. They must have moved on. He was OK.

He fumbled in the hollow where the top stone had been. And there was the pendant, just as Sloper had said it would be. He lifted it out. A leather thong threaded through a polished disc cut from an antler. The stag's head emblem burned onto both sides.

He put the thong around his neck. Now it was his. But retrieving the pendant was the easy part. The difficult bit was what came next: making it back to Thornditch before the hound boys caught up with him. By now, they'd have spread out through the valleys and mountains. They'd be scouring the slopes for any sign of him. If any of them spotted him, the cry would go up and they'd all come running.

The time for speed was over. From now on, it was stealth that mattered most.

First he needed to get his breath back. He sat down on a flat rock with his back against the cairn. Stretched and flexed his legs until the cramp in his calf loosened. His breathing slowed, heart rate slowed.

At eye level, a buzzard circled in the darkening sky then veered off southwards, towards the shelter of valley and woodland.

A few fat drops of rain hit his face and arms. He looked up, hardly believing it. After nearly three months of drought, rain. He lifted his face to it, tasted it on his tongue. It was real, rain falling hard and fast now. Soon the parched mountain streams would run with water again. There'd be green in the valleys instead of browns and dull golds. The bad times were over. The land would heal. It was going to be all right.

He stood and raised his arms to the sky. Suddenly he felt giddy with excitement, the Stag Chase momentarily forgotten as he laughed and spun in the downpour. The rain washed the sweat and dust from his skin.

Clouds piled in from the north. The wind moaned over the rocks.

Ash stopped his joyful dance. He looked towards the horizon, and the clouds blotted out the sun.

TWENTY~EIGHT

The gloom leeched colour from the land. Greyed the scorched grass, dulled the bracken, tarred the rocks with shadow.

Along the eastern horizon a line of enormous boulders hunched like giant crouching beasts under the angry sky.

Shivering with cold, Ash started back down Black Crag.

Halfway down, he slid on a slick of loose stone, feet skidding out from under him. He fell onto gorse. The long needles stabbed into his hand. He scrambled free, stood and pulled needles one by one from his flesh. Beads of blood welled out. Fear ran through him, as if the scent of his blood might bring predators hungering along his trail.

As if in reply, the soughing wind carried the distant baying of the hound boys to him. He stopped to listen, uneasy, wondering if these were real boys or wraiths. Either way, they'd seen him, must have. His heartbeat quickened. Now the chase was really on.

The wind drove the rain into him. Thunder growled. A few seconds later, lightning ripped through the gathering dark.

He set off again, followed a path around the shoulder of the mountain, out of sight of the hounds. He descended more slowly now, placed his feet carefully. He reached a short drop and eased over the edge, hooked his fingers into crevices, pressed himself against stone already slippery with rain. Felt around for toeholds, descended a little further. Halfway down he lost his grip. He landed awkwardly, banged his ankle against a knuckle of rock. He rubbed it, tested his weight on it. Bruised but nothing broken, nothing sprained.

No path here. Instead there was only a dense scrub of heather and gorse, bracken and stunted thorn trees.

He glanced back up towards the summit. In the storm light, Black Crag looked different. Not transformed exactly but somehow more than itself, its features taken to extremes. Its southern flank rose in rocky jags like the hackles of a hyena to its blunt summit. Then it dropped down to the north in a series of huge steps.

The hound boys bayed again, closer this time, their

calls echoed by other boys scattered through the nearby mountains and valleys. They were the hunters and he was the hunted. Suddenly he felt sick with fear.

Breathe. Think.

The rain slanted in, sheets of it, grey and cold.

Without a path to follow, the going was rough. His feet sank into the thick mattress of scratchy heather. Already the skin around his ankles felt raw. He lumbered on, wading through the dense growth, moving from one rocky island to the next.

The rain changed. It became thinner and harder. It stung like grit on his exposed skin. His soaked vest and shorts clung uncomfortably to his body.

At last he came to another path. It was faint, the merest trace. Worn by generations of grazing sheep, leading nowhere in particular. But at least it was a path. Head down under the tilted mask, he ran along it, down into the valley and around Midsummer Tor to where the western end of Stag's Leap rose like a vast petrified wave from the valley floor.

The wind picked up, hammered him with hard howling gusts. Rain swept across the land in chains. It bounced off the rock, off sun-baked mud, off patches of grass, exploded into a fine mist. Raindrops glittered in his eyelashes.

He heard faraway voices again. In the near distance, figures moved through the blur of rain. He crouched in the bracken, watching them through a lattice of fronds. Three of them, hound boys, walking in single file. Flesh and blood boys, solid and steady.

They came out onto the open ground and stopped. Ash froze, held his breath. Any moment now they'd look his way, see him crouching there, bedraggled and pathetic.

The wind carried their voices.

'Are you sure you saw him? Sure he came this way?'

'He must have. There's nowhere else he could go without us seeing him. He must be up on the Leap somewhere.'

'Can't see a damn thing in this rain. We should have run faster. We should have got to him before the storm started.'

'He can't have gone far. Running into that wind's like running into a bloody wall.'

'He's probably hiding around here somewhere, crawled into a hole or hiding behind a rock or something.'

Ash froze. If they started searching, it wouldn't take long for them to find him.

'Split up,' said one of them. 'Scout around.'

Ash hunkered down further, a tight ball in a thicket of bracken. He heard one of them blunder towards him, singing under his breath. *Hush, little stag boy, don't you cry*... The hound boy stopped and stood so close that Ash imagined he could feel the heat from his body, hear the raindrops hitting his skin.

Ash closed his eyes. *If I can't see him then he can't see me.*

All at once, the hound boy turned and crashed away.

Ash opened his eyes, peered through the bracken again.

They were standing together about ten metres away. He could hear the urgency in their voices but he couldn't make out their words. Then one of them gestured down the mountainside. A few seconds later they headed off, loping along like wolves following the scent trail of their prey.

Ash huddled in the hard rain, shivering, blinking water from his eyelashes.

When he was sure they must be too far away to look back and see him, he stood up.

The hound boys were lost to the rain haze but they were still out there somewhere, most likely seeking out others to help them search.

He'd have to move fast.

He'd climbed the northern slope of the Leap with Dad at least a dozen times. It was a slog but straightforward enough, no need for ropes. Even in the sheeting rain, he climbed steadily.

At the top, he stopped. In the storm gloom, he was no longer afraid that the hound boys would see him. He could run the length of the ridge, descend along the path that dropped down past the Cullen farm to the valley, loop around and return to Thornditch from the east.

He set off at a steady trot, stones clacking underfoot, mud spattering up his legs.

He ran half a mile along the ridge.

Then, through the welter of the storm, a figure came towards him.

TWENTY~NINE

A hazy shadow at first, featureless. Then, as the figure came closer, Ash made out more detail. The ragged outline of a hound mask. A muscular body streaked with pale clay.

Somehow he'd already known it would be Mark. The unhurried stride towards him, the lowered head, the arms swinging a little, loose and dangerous. A warrior's walk, not a hunter's.

No point in running now.

Mark stopped a few feet away, facing him. Watched him from behind his mask.

'You're bleeding,' said Mark. 'I can smell it. That's how I found you. I followed the scent of your blood and it led me straight to you.'

'Don't talk crap,' said Ash. 'You're a boy, not a real hound.'

Mark laughed. 'It would be good though, wouldn't it? Tracking you down by the scent of your blood.'

'So how did you find me?'

'I knew you'd come to the Leap.'

'You can't have known. Even I didn't know.'

'And yet here you are.'

'What now?' said Ash.

But he already knew the answer. He was caught. His Stag Chase was over. All that training, everything he'd gone through, it was all for nothing in the end. He wouldn't cross the finishing line in triumph, wouldn't get to wear the antler headdress. Even if Mum got Dad to leave the house and brought him to the finish, there'd be no victory to celebrate. All that was over now. He might as well have given up before the race started, like he'd wanted to.

He didn't even care any more. It was over. He'd failed. That was that.

He took the stag's head pendant from around his neck and held it out to Mark. 'Take it. I'm done. I'm going home.'

'I don't want it.'

'I'm not looking for favours. You caught me, fair and square. You've won and I've lost. Take it.'

'You still don't get it, do you?' said Mark. He

wrenched off his mask, hurled it into the wind. 'I don't care about the stupid pendant. I don't care who wins the race. That's not what it's about.'

Ash tied the leather thong of the pendant around his neck again. He'd hand it in when he came down from the mountain, give it to Sloper, then go home, sleep. But first he had to deal with Mark.

'So what is it about then?'

'You. Me. My dad.' He gazed away, into the gloom. 'My dad, he never should have died. It wasn't his time. It was a mistake. And I have to put things right.'

'By killing me? That's really what you've come here to do?'

Mark smiled, turned his back on Ash, opened his arms. 'Don't you see them?' he said. 'The wraiths? They're all around you. You must have seen them. I know you've seen them. The hound boys from the old days, from the dark times.'

Ash peered into the driving rain. Movement in its depths, blurry shadows advancing. A dozen or more of them, their movements erratic and unnatural. They leaped and twisted, flitted this way and that with a speed and lightness that no flesh-and-blood boy possessed.

The hairs on the back of his neck prickled. 'What do they want?'

'They want the stag boy. You. They want blood and death.'

'Why though? Why me? What for?'

Mark smiled at him, cold and strange. 'It's nothing personal. They're hounds and you're the stag boy. They hunt and kill. It's just what they do. It's all they know.'

'So what are they? The ghosts of medieval psychopaths or something?'

Mark shook his head. 'Like I told you before, in the old days if the hounds caught the stag boy, they'd kill him. A blood offering to the land. Centuries of blood and death and terror, the old ways written into the land, like memories. People tried to forget them, but they won't be forgotten.'

'How do you know all this?'

'Because a few folk refused to forget. They passed it on, father to son, mother to daughter, down the generations. My grandpa told it to my dad and my dad told it to me. That's how I know. The past doesn't go away, Ash Tyler, no matter how much people want it to. It's still all around us. It has an afterlife of its own.'

Ash shivered, still watching the dim shapes of the wraith hound boys moving through the rain.

Mark came closer. Head down, skip, skip, from foot to foot. 'Out here, if you take something then you have to give something back,' he said. 'It's the way of things. Once upon a time, people knew that. That's what the stag boy is supposed to be, a sacrifice to the land in times of hardship. Well, it's a time of hardship now, isn't it? The sheep all slaughtered, the land diseased, my dad dead and other hill farmers going bankrupt, getting kicked off their land. Sometimes we have to go back to the old ways to put things right. Blood for blood, life for life.' He stopped skipping, lifted his head. Eyes bright and fierce behind the mask. 'The stag boy's life in exchange for my dad's.'

The wraiths came closer through the murk. Baying, yelping, howling.

Ash started to back away. 'Your dad's dead,' he said. 'Nothing's going to bring him back.'

'Look around you,' said Mark. 'All those hound boys are dead. But they've come back.'

'No,' said Ash. 'They haven't come back, not really. They're wraiths, ghosts. They're not alive like me and you. Is that what you want? Your dad like one of those howling crazy things out there?'

'Earth and stone needs blood and bone, Ash Tyler. It always has and it always will. It takes life so that it can give life. Life for life. I didn't want it to be you. I told you to pull out of the race. I tried to save you.'

'Then what? You'd sacrifice some other kid instead of me? You've lost it, Mark. You're crazy. Stark staring mad. What the hell happened to you?'

Mark took a step towards him. 'This is what happened. I came out here into the mountains. I thought about my dad. I couldn't stop thinking about him. I walked and walked. I didn't eat for days. I didn't sleep. I walked and I searched and in the end the ghosts came to me from their dead place, hound boys from the ancient days. They were weak then, whispering voices and a breath of mist. But they got stronger every day. They whispered things to me. They told me to kill the birds.'

'The birds?'

Mark nodded. 'Bone Jack's rooks. Kill the birds and take Bone Jack's power. Now he's the weak one, too weak to stop the dead getting through. Bone Jack can't stop the hound boys. He can't stop me bringing back my dad.'

Ash remembered the wolf. That must have come through too, somehow. That was why Bone Jack had come for it. *Back where it belongs*, he had said. Back to Annwn, the Otherworld. But the wolf hadn't been a wraith. It had felt real, solid. He'd run his fingers through its fur, searching for a collar. He'd felt its ribs, felt its hot breath on his skin as he'd dribbled water into its mouth.

Maybe it was different with animals, or it had been dead a shorter time. Or maybe the hound boys weren't as wraithlike as they looked.

He switched his attention back to Mark. 'If Bone Jack can't stop you bringing back your dad, why don't you just go and get him? Why are you out here? Why do you need to kill me?'

Mark shook his head at him. His eyes were wild, dangerous. 'It's how it has to be,' he said. 'Life for life.'

'I don't care about your crazy stuff any more,' said Ash. 'I ran this race for my dad. That's it. Now you've caught me so it's over. Got it? It's over. I'm going home.'

He backed away further. Now the ghost hound boys tore from the gloom, spun and lunged and soared. One of them hurtled past him. He felt the boy's cold airy touch against his skin, breathed in the ancient stink of the grave.

He flinched, shuddered. 'Call them off, Mark,' he said. 'Get them off me!'

Mark shook his head. 'I can't. I don't tell them what to do, and it's not over just because you want it to be.'

The hounds drew back into the rain, regrouped. Endlessly moving, shifting, advancing again, circling, crowding around Ash. They were in front of him, to his side, behind him. One moment they just seemed like boys in masks, boys like him. The next they were wraiths, rags of mist veiling scorched bone, lipless grins, empty eye sockets.

Ash hurled himself in the only direction left open to him. Scrambled over scree, slipping on wet black stone as shiny as plastic. Across springy turf that squelched underfoot, on to rain-slick rock.

He glanced back. Mark was standing where he'd left him, hands on hips, watching him. As if he knew it wasn't worth chasing, knew Ash couldn't get away.

Ash ran harder, faster.

Again the hound boys advanced through the rain. Still spinning and leaping but moving forward slowly, as if it didn't really matter that he'd bolted. As if they, like Mark, already knew that he couldn't get away.

Rain swept over the ridge. The wind screamed. And through it came Mark, and the wind's scream was his scream, and so too was the beating of Ash's heart and the pounding of his blood, all one squalling primal shriek.

Mark flew at him. Smashed into him, seized him, beat him down onto rock and pooling rainwater. Ash threw out wild panicky punches. He twisted free, rolled over, scrambled away on all fours. He got to his feet, winded and gasping for breath. But Mark wasn't done yet. He cannoned into Ash again, a low tackle that sent Ash reeling backwards.

Ash hollered at him through the wind and rain.

Mark came at him a third time. Again the impact shunted Ash backwards. Then he realised. That was what Mark wanted, to push him back and back until he fell off the edge, like the other stag boy must have fallen, flailing down onto the splintered rocks below.

Ash veered away from the edge. He stood gasping in the rain, head down, facing Mark. 'You can't do this,' he said. 'Your dad wouldn't want you to do this.'

'You don't know what my dad would want.'

'I do,' said Ash. 'I know. Those things, those wraiths, came after my dad when he was the stag boy twenty years ago. They got into his head and because of them he ended up on the Leap and about to jump off. I don't know how but they made him want to jump. But your dad saw my dad standing there, right at the edge, and he pulled him back. He saved my dad's life.'

'Liar!' screamed Mark. He came at Ash again. But this time Ash sidestepped, flung his arms around Mark, clung to him. They lurched and wrestled, a weird dance in the howling chaos of the storm. 'You know it's true,' said Ash. The words came out like sobs. 'You know. You won't kill me. You're not a killer.'

And then it stopped. Mark stopped. Let go of Ash. He stood there in the weltering storm, his chest heaving, his eyes bright with tears.

But the hound boys came again, hurtling with the storm wind. Smashing into Mark, into Ash.

Ash staggered. Off balance, the world tilting, the wind battering about him. He felt Mark's hand close about his wrist, felt Mark brace and strain and take his weight to haul him back from the edge. But there was nothing beneath his feet any more. He plunged through the wild air, and Mark was still holding on, falling with him.

Then came the hard slam onto rock, a quake of pain, the taste of blood in his mouth, and bottomless dark.

THIRTY

He opened his eyes and stared straight up. Sky churning with dark clouds. Rain spiking his face like nails.

For a few moments he had no idea where he was.

Then he remembered falling.

He shifted his weight. Pain knifed in his shoulder. More pain in both elbows, his right hip, his head, his ribs. Gritting his teeth, he hauled himself up into a sitting position. He ran his fingers through his hair. The stag mask must have come off in the fall, torn away by the wind. His hand came away bloody.

But he was alive. Being dead couldn't hurt this much.

A sob shook through him. He felt it, heard it, but it seemed to have nothing to do with him. A reaction of his body. His mind hadn't caught up yet.

Mark was lying nearby. He was on his side with one arm twisted unnaturally beneath him. Eyes closed. His mouth slightly open. A trickle of blood, diluted by rain-water, ran down his forehead and dripped from the bridge of his nose.

He wasn't moving.

He looked dead.

Ash stared at him for a long time.

They'd landed on a ledge. To his right was a five-metre wall of rock. To his left was a sheer drop. Far below, splinters of black granite stabbed up through a sea of gloomy rain-mist.

Ash rolled his injured shoulder, stretched his arm upwards and then out. A spasm of pain but it was bearable. He checked the rest of his body: bruises, cuts, scrapes. Nothing broken, nothing dislocated.

He felt for the stag's head pendant, as if it was a talisman. But it was gone from around his neck, lost to the storm and the darkness.

He crawled towards Mark. He tugged Mark's hand. It felt cold and limp, wet with rain. 'Mark,' he said. 'Wake up, Mark. Come on, wake up.'

Not a flicker.

He pressed two fingers to Mark's throat to see if he had a pulse. At first he couldn't feel anything except Mark's chilled skin against his own. Then he felt a throb of life, faint but unmistakable.

'Come on, Mark. Wake up. Please.'

Mark groaned, coughed, spat blood and rainwater. He rolled onto his back and screamed.

'Don't move,' said Ash. 'You're injured. I think your arm is broken. Maybe more.'

Mark's breath came in quick dry gasps. 'What happened?' he said. His voice was a whisper.

'The hound boys slammed into us. I was too close to the edge. You tried to hold on to me but we both fell. We landed on this ledge. We were lucky.'

'Lucky, yeah,' said Mark. Turned his face away.

Ash shook in great slow shudders. Yet his thoughts were cold and clear, bright as ice.

He waited it out.

When the shudders stopped, he took off the backpack. He emptied its contents between his outstretched legs. Found the whistle and blew it. The wind ripped away the thin sound. Even if anyone was out searching for them yet, they'd never hear the whistle in this storm.

Useless.

He slid the empty backpack under Mark's head as a pillow. Mark moaned, his eyes shut.

Ash sat with his back to the rock face. He drew up his knees, hugged himself into a tight ball. Rain beat on his skull, slid down his back, pooled underneath him. He stared into the murky distance. He was an ant, an atom. There was nothing he could do about anything any more. The storm would rage. Night would come. If they survived until the morning, perhaps the search-and-rescue team would find them.

Perhaps.

Or Mark would die.

Ash couldn't let that happen. No way.

He couldn't go down the rock face, not without ropes and proper equipment. The drop was too far, sheer and hazardous. But maybe he could climb back up to the top, fetch help.

He stood up. He walked the length of the ledge, feeling for handholds and footholds in the rock face. All he found were cracks too narrow to slide his fingers into, nubbins so smooth and slick with rain that his feet slithered off them straightaway.

An angle of rock sticking out, about half a metre above his head. He jumped for it, reaching up with his good arm, fingers scraping the rock face a hand's breadth below it. He jumped again, and again, sobbing with the effort. But there wasn't enough strength left in him and he knew that even if he managed to reach it, he was too weak to pull himself up.

It was impossible.

He sank back down, defeated. He watched the endless fall of rain, drops shattering in diamond bursts on the rock in front of him. He watched dark clouds as tall as mountains heave and collide and tear apart. The brief brilliant burn of distant lightning. He slept a little, woke with a start, slept again, woke.

It was getting dark now.

Someone was watching him.

He lifted his head.

A boy, sitting at the furthest end of the ledge. An impossible stag boy with his hair in spikes, his face and body streaked with white and black clay.

Ash laughed out loud at the craziness of it. A hallucination or another dream, that was all. He struggled to keep his eyes open but his eyelids felt too heavy, the pull of sleep too strong.

When he woke again, the stag boy was still there. His clay-painted face gleamed. Rain rolled down his cheeks like tears. His charcoal-shadowed eyes were deep, dark and serious.

'Why are you here?' said Ash. 'What do you want?'

The stag boy was silent, watching him.

'I've seen you before,' said Ash. 'Up on the top, a couple of weeks ago, running from the hound boys.'

The stag boy watched.

'You're dead,' said Ash. 'You're centuries dead.'

The wind snatched away his words. But, as if the stag boy had heard enough, he stood up. Still holding Ash's gaze. Then, slowly and deliberately, he turned to face the rock wall. He went closer to it. Then he reached up, hooked his fingers into a tiny fissure and started to climb.

'Come down,' said Ash weakly. 'It's too dangerous. It's impossible. Come back.'

Ash grinned like a fool, shook his head. Talking to a dream, warning a ghost. Nothing was dangerous for a ghost.

The stag boy kept reaching and climbing and Ash kept watching until the boy hauled himself over the top and disappeared from sight.

Gone.

Just a dream. Just a ghost. Or some sort of memory imprinted on the land. Maybe Mark was right and that's what ghosts are, Ash thought. Land memories, visual echoes of the past. Terrible things had happened out here and the land remembered. *Earth and stone, fire and ash, blood and bone.* They became part of its substance, its dreaming, its nightmares. And sometimes they broke through and became real again.

He remembered the book he'd taken from Bone Jack's bothy. The poem printed in it.

> *I have been in a multitude of shapes,*
> *Before I assumed a consistent form.*

His thoughts jarred, jammed, broke apart. He raised his face to the darkening sky. Opened his mouth and tasted the rain.

> *I have been a tear in the air,*
> *I have been the dullest of stars.*

Not a star in the sky now. Not one.

> *I will believe when it is apparent.*

Get it together. Think. Move.

He shook tears of rainwater from his eyes.

What is apparent?

That long ago the hounds had chased the stag boy up onto the Leap. And the stag boy had fallen. Fallen and landed on the ledge, just like Ash.

And he'd climbed back up.

I will believe when it is apparent . . .

If the stag boy had climbed the rock face, that meant Ash could too.

'This happened to you,' he said to the empty air where the stag boy had been, to the dark, to the storm. 'You fell and you survived. You climbed back up to the top.'

He struggled to his feet. Shivering, stiff with cold. Every inch of his body felt battered and bruised. He stamped warmth back into his muscles, flexed and stretched. He ate two of the energy bars, washed them down with bottled water.

He crouched next to Mark. 'I'm going to climb up out of here,' he told him. 'I'm going to fetch help. And I'm going to come back for you.'

Mark's eyes opened a crack.

Then Ash stood where the stag boy had stood. The ledge was narrow here, no more than an arm's length between the rock face and the drop. He reached up where the stag boy had reached, found a fissure in the rock just big enough to hook his fingers into. The way the stag boy had shown him, the way Dad had taught him. It came easily now, following the stag boy's route, using the training Dad had given him. He felt calm, clear-headed. He searched for a toehold, found a small jag of rock, then a hollow for his other foot, then another handhold.

His bruised shoulder knotted with pain as it took his weight. He grunted and ignored it, hung on, reached up with his free hand for another crack in the rock. The wind slammed him against the rock face then tore at him. He clung on by his fingertips. The side of his face pressed against wet rock. Every sinew in his body strained. If he fell from here, there was no chance he'd land on the ledge again. He'd fall all the way down to the far-below rocks. He'd shatter.

His head spun with a horror of heights.

He held himself very still, concentrated on the rock face, steadied his breathing. The next handhold, the next foothold.

Again.

On and on, up and up.

Then he reached up and there was no more rock, just air and then rough grass under his hand. He dug his fingers into wet gritty turf. Another heave and he was halfway over the edge of the Leap. He clawed at mud and loose stone. His fingers scraped through wet grass. He slid backwards. Feet scrabbling against the rock face for a toehold. Then he found one, shunted himself upwards again. This time his hand closed around a tangle of thin roots. He clung on, pushed and pulled, got one knee up on the edge and hauled himself over.

Limp as a rag, he lay on his back. Sharp stones dug into his ribs. He sucked air greedily then rolled over, away from the edge. His eyes wide open. Skull full of the moan and boom of the wind.

The hound boys were nowhere in sight.

He laughed with relief.

He'd made it.

But it wasn't over yet. Mark was still down there, injured, perhaps even dying by now. He had to find help.

He got to his feet and stood swaying, squinting into the battering wind. In the far distance, the skyline glowed fiery red through the murk of rain. He frowned at it. Not sunset. This was different, a blazing line like a tide of lava flowing towards him.

Weird, and still a long way off. There were more urgent things to worry about. He stumbled down the slope, fast as he could. Twice he fell, knees cracking down on the rocky ground. Hauled himself upright again, staggered on.

Three miles back to Thornditch. The darkness thickening into night, the storm smashing against the mountains. As weak as he was, it could take him until morning to get there. There was a good chance he wouldn't make it at all.

But there was nothing else he could do.

One foot in front of the other. Like Dad always used to say. He'd crawl if he had to. Just keep going.

His eyes closed. He lost his balance, staggered sideways, opened his eyes again.

Something moved further down the slope. Ash stopped and peered through the rain. Now he saw them. Hound boys, pale as moonlight. They lifted their masked heads, sniffed the wind. Their eerie shriek-yelps rose above the storm.

He shivered with fear.

Too exhausted to run and nowhere to run to anyway.

He stood still and watched them come.

THIRTY~ONE

They came at Ash like a breaking wave. They raced and tumbled through the misty darkness. Their howls filled his ears, filled his skull until he couldn't think of anything else. Their bony fingers scraped over his skin. With each touch, he grew colder, weaker, until his trembling legs could no longer hold him upright and he sagged to the ground.

He knelt there in the hard rain. No strength left. Nothing more he could do.

'You're not real,' he whispered to them. But they were. As real as the wolf, as real as the rocks and the storm.

His raised his head, peered into the rain. Ahead lay burnt ground, leafless bone-white trees stark against a plain of blackened rock.

Not real. It couldn't be real.

Get up, said a voice in his mind.

Callie's voice.

He blinked rain from his eyelashes. 'Callie?'

A whisper.

No one there. She was in his head, nowhere else. He was alone.

Except for the hound boys.

Get up.

He pushed against the ground, against gravity, against the dead weight of his own body.

Get up, get up.

He pushed again. He stood swaying in the wind, head down, looking out over a scorched landscape that should not be there. The distant rim of fire was fiercer now, getting closer all the time.

The hound boys circled, pressed in close again. He heard the click-clack of their bones, the moan of the wind through their fleshless skulls. The wind ripped trails of smoke from their grinning mouths.

The rain on his skin seemed as dark as blood. The air thick with smoke, bitter and foul.

And the rain kept falling.

He gathered himself. Hollered and barged into the hound boys, felt them crunch and fold. Then he was through them, out into the open.

Along the skyline, a wall of fire raced towards them.

Wildfire.

Not real, not real. None of this is real.

Around him the hound boys yapped and bayed.

Ash froze. His gaze fixed on the wildfire. A thorn tree exploded into flames. Dark smoke and gritty ash swirled in the wind. It raked his throat, brought stinging tears to his eyes. He coughed and retched.

None of this is real.

But he wasn't sure. Maybe it was real, after all. If the smoke could choke him, then surely the fire could burn him.

Panic ran through him. Ahead lay the inferno and behind him the slope rose steeply to the sheer drop of Stag's Leap. He was trapped.

Unless he could somehow climb back down to the ledge where Mark was. Maybe on the ledge they'd be safe from the fire.

He started to run, stumbling over the lumpy ground, slow, so slow, because there was no strength left in him, nothing keeping him on his feet now except raw terror.

Halfway back up to the top, he switched direction, cut across towards the ledge where he and Mark had fallen.

Instantly the hound boys came after him. They clamoured and swarmed, blocked his path. He veered away but they flowed around him, blocked him again.

He yelled and swung wild blows at them, but he was too exhausted, too weak.

This time they didn't fold and fall back, didn't let him through.

'Why are you doing this?' he said. Teeth chattering with fear and cold. His smoke-roughened voice no more than a whisper. 'What do you want?'

They were silent behind their masks but he knew the answer, in all its terrible simplicity, knew they only wanted to kill him, the stag boy, and that there was nothing more to them than this one overwhelming urge. There could be no pleading with them; there was nothing he could offer them.

In the distance beyond them, fire raced between the dirty sky and the dark land.

The wind blew hot.

He sank to his knees. Nowhere to run. Even if there was, he'd no strength left. Nothing to do except wait for the wildfire to roll over him. Wait to die.

He gazed into a blazing shimmer of orange heat.

And something moved in its depths.

Something as black as shadow, moving fast, swift and low. It reached the fire line, bunched and bounded clear.

Ash rubbed tears and grit from his eyes, peered past the hounds, through the smoke and fire-flung shadows.

The wolf.

It leaped onto a boulder and stood stock-still. Impossibly, it seemed strong and healthy, a far cry from the dying beast he'd found in the mountains just days ago. Yet it was undoubtedly the same animal. It watched him with bright amber eyes, its head lowered.

Behind it came a wild figure, untouched by the flames, striding out over the scorched ground, through smoke and storm. Long coat snapping out in the wind, gaunt face etched in shadow under his wide-brimmed hat. Eyes full of murder.

Bone Jack.

Ash blinked and stared, half blinded by smoke. Now the raw cries of rooks filled his ears. Dark within dark, against a spitting wall of flame. The wind shrieked.

Earth and stone, fire and ash, blood and bone.

As one, the hounds turned their dead faces towards Bone Jack.

Wild man, raggedy man, birdman.

Bone Jack whirled and shattered. Broke apart into wing, feather, beak until there was no longer any semblance of a man there, only rooks like black rags against the screen of wildfire. They tumbled and swooped. Every wing beat, every thrust of beak and claw, every serrated cry, drove the hound boys back.

The hounds howled, flailed at the birds.

The birds kept coming.

Smoke like a dense dark fog, sparking with fire. The hounds were shadows flickering within it, the parched grass igniting beneath them. Fire spat at them, danced up their tattered clothes, their clay-spiked hair. Briefly they whirled there, scarecrows of fire and blackened bone with charred grins, smoke misting around them. Then the wall of flame collapsed over them and they were gone.

Ash stood up. Coughs heaved up out of him. His eyes were raw with smoke.

The rooks flew back out of the fire. They hurtled towards each other, flocked into a single fluid shadow that darkened and deepened and shrank until there was only Bone Jack there, whole again, striding through swirling smoke with the wildfire rearing behind him and the wolf at his side.

Ash turned away.

Someone else, a little way up the slope, pale in the deepening darkness. The stag boy.

He was pacing, head down. Four quick strides out, sharp turn, four quick strides back. He stopped, watched Ash through his mask.

Bone Jack coming out of the shadows, moving fast, his gaze locked on the stag boy.

'You've got to go now,' said Ash to the stag boy. 'Go on, run. Get away.'

The stag boy paced. One, two, three, four, turn. And now the wolf paced with him, shadowed him, matched him step for step.

'Run!' But it was too late. Bone Jack was already there, spinning out wild nets of bird and shadow.

The stag boy stopped pacing. He stared at Bone Jack. 'Come on, lad,' said Bone Jack.

The stag boy leaned into the wind, took a step forward.

'Not him!' yelled Ash to Bone Jack. 'He saved my life! He's not one of them!'

Another step. The stag boy was airy as a ghost.

'Time to go home,' said Bone Jack.

The stag boy already dissolving like mist, the dark land visible through him, the black wind howling through him. He reached out his hand towards Bone Jack and Bone Jack took it in his own, pulled the spectral stag boy to him, embraced him.

Then the boy was gone. No one there except Bone Jack, striding again towards Ash through the churning smoke, the wildfire furnace-bright behind him.

Ash sagged back to the ground. No strength, no hope, nothing. 'What have you done?' he whispered. 'I don't understand. What have you done?'

Bone Jack crouched in front of him. 'Hush now, lad,' he said.

'He saved me,' Ash said. 'What have you done to him? Is he dead?'

'He's centuries dead, lad,' said Bone Jack. 'They all are. He had to go back. They've all to go back.'

'You should have taken them back days ago. Then none of this would have happened.'

'Ain't that simple.'

'Why not? Because Mark killed the rooks?'

'Not that.'

'What then?'

'You ever tried catching mist with your bare hands? The hounds are like that. Most years they stay that way then, like mist, they fade to nowt in the morning sun. Death and drought made them strong this year. I waited until they were at their strongest, until they had weight and substance and they'd run you to ground. Sometimes you have to let things run their course before you make your move.'

'You got them though, in the end.'

'Aye, I did. Now hush, lad. You've got to get up, get moving. You've got to get help for your friend.'

'Mark.'

'Aye, Mark. Up then, lad, and on.'

Ash got to his feet, stood swaying in the storm.

'The storm's blowing the wildfire westwards,' said Bone Jack. 'So stay on this path, come down the eastern side of the Leap.'

'How can there be rain and fire at the same time?'

'Because the land's so dry. Deep-down dry. Once wildfire's got a hold, it's hot as a thousand furnaces. Evaporates the rain before it even hits the ground. It'll take more than a few hours of rain to stop a wildfire.'

'OK then,' said Ash.

He straightened. He looked round for Bone Jack but Bone Jack was gone again.

Ash took a step forward, then another.

THIRTY~TWO

Ash walked but nothing worked any more. His legs were stone-heavy. He could barely lift his feet clear of the rough ground. The land lurched sideways. He slumped down onto the wet grass and lay there, too exhausted to get up again. He could lie here, he could close his eyes, he could drift away, sleep or die. He had no strength to care any more.

Shouts below. A familiar voice.

Ash opened his eyes.

Dad, running out of the wind and rain.

'Go back,' Ash said. The words a whisper, sticking in his raw throat. 'Go back down, Dad. There's wildfire. There's ghosts. It's not safe.'

But Dad couldn't hear and Ash knew he wouldn't have turned back even if he could. He kept coming.

Blinding white glare of torchlight. Ash flinched, turned

his face away. And all at once Dad was there with him, holding him so tight it hurt, Dad shaking as much as Ash was.

'He was here,' whispered Ash. 'Bone Jack was here. And they've all burned and he's gone into the night.'

'Who's burned? Who's gone?'

'The hound boys. They all burned in the wildfire. Dad, we need to get off the mountain. We need to get help.'

'No one burned,' said Dad. Voice taut as wire. 'The hound boys all came back to Thornditch. Only you and Mark Cullen missing. And I've got you now. The wind's blowing the wildfire westwards, so we can get down the eastern side, get behind it. It's going to be all right.'

Then Callie was there too, running up to them. Her face pale and anxious.

'What the hell?!' said Dad. 'Callie, I told you to wait with the others down in Thornditch. It's too dangerous up here.'

Callie stared blankly at him, then switched her gaze to Ash. 'Where's Mark?' she said. 'He didn't come down from the mountains. I asked everyone but no one's seen him.'

'We fell off the Leap,' said Ash. 'We landed on a ledge. Mark's injured. I climbed up to get help.'

'How badly injured?'

'I don't know. I think his arm is broken, and maybe he banged his head. He's alive though. He talked to me.'

'Where is he?'

Ash nodded his head towards where they'd fallen. Immediately, Callie took off.

Dad swore. 'Callie! Get back here! We'll work out what to do about Mark in a minute!'

But Callie didn't answer and didn't come back.

'Bloody hell,' said Dad. 'That's all I need. One kid half dead with exhaustion, another one fallen off a cliff and now Callie's gone walkabout.'

His voice jittery, full of panic.

'It's OK, Dad,' said Ash. 'She'll be all right. She knows the mountains better than anyone. Even better than you.'

'All right,' said Dad. He drew a long, slow breath, squared his shoulders. 'All right. First things first. Let's get you sorted out.'

He shrugged out of his rucksack, opened it, pulled out a foil blanket and wrapped it around Ash.

Everything in fragments. Dad hugging him, stubble rough against his skin. The tension in Dad's body, in his voice. Then hot sweet tea from a thermos flask. Chunks of flapjack. A little of Ash's strength started to come back.

He looked at Dad. 'Dad,' he said. His voice shaking as

much as his body. 'We have to find the rescue team so they can get Mark off that ledge.'

'The rescue team headed off towards Black Crag. They won't be back yet, and getting around the wildfire will slow them down.'

'Why didn't you go with them? Why did you come up onto the Leap instead?'

Dad smiled uneasily. 'Just a wild guess.'

'It was a good guess.'

'I went to Tom's grave before I went to the start of the race,' said Dad. 'Like you did.'

'Mum told you.'

'Yeah. There was a photograph on the grave: me and Tom and Callie and you and Mark when you were little. We were up on the Leap.'

'Yeah, I saw that too.'

'When you didn't come down from the mountains with the others, I knew something was wrong and I couldn't get that photo out of my mind. It seemed like a message or something, a message from Tom. That picture of us all up on the Leap, then that day when I was the stag boy and Tom saved my life up here. Stag's Leap. So I came, and here you are.'

'Here we are.'

'Feeling any better now?'

'Yeah, a bit. But we have to help Mark, Dad.'

'Yeah, I know,' said Dad. 'I'll try calling Mountain Rescue, see if they'll send another team out to us.'

He tried his mobile phone, frowned. 'No signal.'

'There's never a signal out here,' said Ash. 'It's a black spot.'

'No phones then,' said Dad. 'Right. It'll take us about an hour to get back down to the road. Maybe longer in these conditions and with you so exhausted. Could be two hours and the same again to get the team back up here. That's minimum, and assuming the wind keeps the fire to the west of us. Mark's injured. He'll be exhausted and wet too. No kit with him. He might not last that long.'

Dad was talking too fast again, panicking again.

'Dad,' said Ash, 'slow down. Please.'

'You told Callie that Mark was conscious when you left him. Do you think he can hang on down there for a few hours while we get help?'

'I don't know,' said Ash. 'He's in a bad way. I don't think so, no.'

'OK,' said Dad. 'I don't think we can risk it. He's injured and he'll likely get hypothermic as well in this rain, with night setting in. We need to bring him up now, ourselves, then get him off the mountain and to hospital as quick as we can. I brought my climbing gear, just in case you'd fallen somewhere. We can do it.'

Of course. Dad, the army officer, the mountain man, the climber. He'd come to rescue Ash in the mountains so he'd come prepared. Still the same old Dad deep inside, in spite of everything. For a moment, Ash felt safe, as if Dad could do anything, save him, save Mark, save all of them.

Except he also knew Dad could lose it at any moment, freak out, run away, hide.

But he didn't. Instead he said, 'I need you to show me exactly where Mark is. Think you can manage that?'

Ash nodded. 'Yeah.'

Dad helped him to his feet. He stood swaying, gathering himself. Then he looked around. 'Callie,' he said. He looked up at the Leap. 'Where did she go? I can't see her.'

They called her name.

The full moon burned through a gap in the clouds.

Then Ash saw her. She was standing at the edge of Stag's Leap. A wild creature of moonlight and shadow, her dark hair flying in the wind. 'She's up there, Dad.'

Dad hauled him upright. They set off towards her. The wind in their faces. Ash half delirious with exhaustion, his body bruised and battered and aching all over. But none of that mattered. He just kept going.

'Callie,' said Dad, 'get away from the edge before you fall down there too. Please.'

She didn't answer, didn't move. She kept her back to them, kept staring down over the edge.

'That's where Mark is,' said Ash. 'Right below where Callie's standing. The ledge is about five metres down.'

Dad went and stood next to Callie. 'It's OK,' he said to her. Gentle, the panic gone from his voice again. 'I'm going to go down there and bring him back up. But I can't do it on my own. You and Ash will have to help me. Are you up to doing that?'

Slowly she turned to look at him. 'Yes,' she said. 'Of course. Just tell me what to do.'

Dad lay down and stuck his head out over the edge. 'Not too bad,' he said. 'A straight drop, about five metres, just like Ash said. The ledge looks pretty wide where Mark's lying.'

Then Dad was on his feet again. The wind gusted and Ash swayed again, braced himself.

Dad stood in front of him. 'Still feeling OK?'

'Yeah. Just tired. Really tired.'

'No wonder. Are you starting to warm up now?'

'Yeah, a bit.'

'How on earth did you climb up that rock face without a rope? It looks sheer from the top.'

Ash shrugged and looked down. 'There's handholds, toeholds. I just sort of did it, the way you taught me.'

'Amazing,' said Dad. 'Really. You did brilliantly. I'm proud of you.'

'Thanks.'

'Listen, Mark's not moving. He's either too weak or he's unconscious. So I'm going to go down there and between us we're going to get him up. I'll take the spare harness for Mark and rig the ropes so you can help me by taking some of Mark's weight as I bring him back up. OK? Do you think you can handle it?'

'Yeah, I can handle it.'

'Callie?'

'Me too.'

'All right then.'

'Dad,' said Ash, 'suppose it's like the other day when we went fishing and you thought there were snipers? Suppose you get flashbacks again?'

'I'm OK,' said Dad. 'I'm keeping it together. I've got a list in my head, all the things we have to do. The ropes and the harnesses, abseil down, bring Mark back up with me, then get us all off this mountain without running straight into the wildfire. I can do it. OK?' He smiled. 'Besides, you and Callie can just haul me back up if I start flipping out.'

'That your idea of a joke, Dad?'

'Yeah. Don't worry. It's going to be OK.'

'What do you want us to do?'

'Stay a couple of metres back from the edge. I'll set up the ropes and I'll need you to start pulling when I give the signal. Pull slow and steady, don't yank the rope, OK?'

Ash nodded. Exhaustion washed through him again. His vision blurred and his eyelids slid shut. He forced them open, focused his eyes. Dad was already pulling his climbing gear from his rucksack. Ash watched as he fixed the anchors, clipped himself into his harness, rolled out ropes.

Dad handed him a pair of gloves and Ash took hold of the rope.

'OK,' said Dad. 'My rope is anchored so you don't need to worry about that. The rope you're holding will take some of Mark's weight so you'll need to be ready. I'll give you a shout but pay attention to the rope in case you don't hear me. When you feel it go taut, start pulling steadily like I told you. Ready?'

'Ready.'

Then Dad went over the edge of the Leap.

THIRTY~THREE

It seemed to Ash that he fell asleep over and over, asleep on his feet, and that each time he woke everything was almost exactly the same. Hours passed, months, years, centuries, and nothing changed. The rope in his gloved hands, the rain still falling, and the wind in his face. There was no weight on the rope yet, but that would come.

The wildfire moving westwards away from them. Dad still over the edge, swinging down the rock face into a storm.

He was too tired to make sense of it any more. All he wanted was to sleep but he couldn't, not yet. Not until all this was over.

He glanced back at Callie.

'Mark's still alive,' said Callie. 'Isn't he?'

'I think so. I'm sure he is.'

'He is,' she said.

It hit him then that Mark was all she had left in the world. Her parents dead. Grandpa Cullen in hospital, maybe going to pull through or maybe not. No one else. Just her and Mark. And Mark's grief, the madness of it, had eclipsed hers, left her desolate on the sideline.

He heard Dad shout.

'OK, pull,' said Ash. 'Slow and steady, like Dad said.'

He tilted his weight back, bracing against the rope, pulled hand over hand. Behind him, Callie took up the slack.

And everything hurt. His muscles taut with pain, his legs and arms trembling.

It seemed like an age passed before he saw Dad clamber up over the edge, turn and reach down, then haul Mark up and over. They sprawled onto the flat ground.

Ash let go of the rope and went to them.

Mark was conscious but loose as a rag doll, his face gaunt with pain. As carefully as they could, Ash and Callie dragged him away from the edge.

'You're alive,' said Callie. A whisper, like she was afraid to say it, couldn't quite believe it.

And Dad unstrapping himself from the harness, pulling up the dangling ropes. Then fidgeting, pacing, all edgy now. 'He's in a bad way,' he said. Talking too fast.

'His shoulder's smashed up and there could be any number of other problems. Head injury, spinal injury, internal bleeding, hypothermia. Anything. We should have a stretcher, a helicopter. We need a damn helicopter. Where the hell is the helicopter?'

'They don't know where we are, remember,' said Ash. 'They don't know where we are and we've no way of telling them so we have to get him down the mountain ourselves. What do we do, Dad? You need to tell us what to do. You can do your freak-out thing after we've got him to hospital. All right?'

Dad stopped pacing. He drew a deep shaky breath. 'OK,' he said. 'I'm OK. You're right. A stretcher. I need the rope and a bivi bag.'

Ash watched as Dad looped rope on the ground, lay a bivi bag on top of it, then another foil blanket.

Carefully they lifted Mark onto it. He sobbed with pain but didn't scream, didn't try to make them stop.

They wrapped him in the foil and then the bivi bag, then Dad laced the ropes around so Mark was cocooned.

'No trees up here,' said Dad. 'It's the best I can do without poles. How are you doing, Mark?'

'I'm OK,' said Mark. His voice barely a whisper.

'We'll get you down as quickly and safely as we can,' said Dad. 'I promise.'

Then Dad took hold of the front and Ash and Callie took the other end between them, slipping their hands under and through the looped rope, and they set off down the eastern slope of the Leap.

THIRTY~FOUR

Ash walked. He walked in the footsteps of long-dead shepherds and hunters, warriors and poets, pedlars and wanderers, lovers, wise women, outlaws, rebels. He felt them all around him, as if the centuries that separated him from them were vapour-thin.

The banshee wind screamed in his ears.

He dreamed the names of scarp and dip and rise and boulder, and they sang through him. The story of the land, written in rock and blood and wraith. Through Silent Hollow and the long shallow trough of Hound-grave. Past Burntwood, where no trees grew; past the Keening Stone, a big teardrop of rock with a smooth round hole that the wind wailed through.

Ash raised his face into the storm.

He glanced at Callie, walking next to him. At Dad ahead. At Mark, swaddled in the bivi bag, his face ghost pale.

He looked to his right and saw Bone Jack.

'Are you really here?' he said.

'Really here.'

'Can they see you too? Dad and Callie and Mark?'

'Mebbe.'

Ash kept walking. Tired beyond tired. He scarcely felt it any more. He zoned in and out. He was borne along by storm and gravity, by willpower, by some ancient instinct of his body.

In the distance, the wildfire was a line of dirty orange that surged and shimmered.

His mind drifted into dreams. He was running barefoot through steady rain, along mountain paths claggy with mud. In this dream, someone ran beside him, but when he turned to see who it was, there was no one there.

Ash stumbled, caught himself. Looked up. The bitter smell of smoke filled his nose and mouth.

'We've been walking for hours,' he said to Bone Jack. 'We've hardly got anywhere.'

'It's only been a few minutes,' said Bone Jack. 'Not hours. Keep on, lad.'

Ash walked. And the world seemed faraway and nothing to do with him, like he didn't belong to it any more.

On.

He watched the wildfire. It seemed brighter, closer. The wind changing direction, driving it towards them again. A roaring tide of fire, eating up the land, smoke rolling over it like low cloud. Rain couldn't stop it. Men couldn't stop it. The land would burn until there was nothing left to burn.

'Are we going to die?' said Ash. His teeth chattered though he wasn't cold any more. 'Are we going to get down off this mountain?'

Bone Jack didn't answer. Ash looked across at him but he was gone, vanished into the night. Maybe he'd never really been there at all.

'Dad,' said Ash. 'The wildfire.'

'I know,' said Dad. 'Keep going. We'll make it.'

And there was only Ash, Dad, Callie and Mark, and a choking blizzard of rain and ember and ash and the wildfire beyond it like the end of the world.

'Keep going,' said Dad. His head bent into the storm, trudging on, steady, relentless.

And then they were past it, the wildfire hungering southwards while they skirted its charred and smouldering flank.

THIRTY~FIVE

There were lights in the valley. Torches, and the head-lamps of cars. Men in red mountain jackets and hard hats ran up to meet them. They brought a proper stretcher, unswaddled Mark, fitted braces to his back and neck and took him away. Blue lights flashing, a siren wailing. Ash watched through his eyelashes. Then Mum was there too, hugging him so hard he could hardly breathe. They put him in the back of a Land Rover ambulance. Voices. Warmth. Mum and Dad standing at the door, watching him. The growl of an engine. A paramedic checking him over. A blood-pressure band tightening around his arm. The door closed. The ambulance bumped down the track.

Ash drifted in and out of sleep.

A white glare. White walls. Bright steel. A metallic rattling noise.

Faces he didn't recognise. A nurse smiling at him. More voices.

A bed in a big half-dark room. He curled up on his side, in the deep warmth of blankets, and slept again.

Woke to daylight.

'All right?' said Mum. 'My love, my precious boy. All right?'

'Mum,' he said. His mind still fogged with sleep. 'What time is it?'

She smiled. 'I'm not sure. About ten o'clock, I think.'

'In the morning?'

'Yes, darling, in the morning.'

The smell of antiseptic. On the wall behind her there was a tall white cabinet, a washbasin, double doors. He looked around. In a bed opposite, a man in his twenties slept propped against several pillows.

At the other end of the room, two more beds. Both empty.

'I'm in hospital,' he said. His voice was a rough whisper, his throat dry and sore.

'Don't you remember?'

'Yes,' he said. 'Sort of. Bits of it anyway.'

'You were suffering from exhaustion and mild expo-sure so they kept you in overnight. They think you might have slight concussion too, and you'll have a sore throat and a cough for a few days from the smoke. You've got some nasty cuts and bruises as well but nothing broken. You were lucky. You could have been killed.'

'I wasn't though.' He could hardly believe it. 'I'm here, I'm alive.'

'You were lucky.'

'It wasn't luck. It was...' Mark. The stag boy. Bone Jack. But he couldn't tell Mum about that stuff. 'Dad,' he said. 'Dad found us and brought us down from the mountain.'

'I know. I was there when you came down.' She smiled. 'The doctor gave you the all-clear to come home today, so long as you promise to rest.'

'I will. Where's Dad?'

'He was here most of the night. He was exhausted himself but he sat with you for hours. We both did.'

'Did he flip out again?' said Ash.

'Yes, a bit. All the strain. The hospital, you know. Mr Sloper gave him a lift home.'

'Right. Dad came to the Stag Chase in the end though, didn't he? I mean, before he knew something had gone wrong in the mountains? He came to see me run?'

'Yes, he did.'

'He wasn't afraid.'

'He was,' she said. 'But he came anyway. He wanted

to stop off at Tom Cullen's grave, just like you did, and you'd already set off by the time we arrived. We waited, so we'd be there when you finished. Then later, when we realised you were missing and there was a storm, he went into army mode. Had to do something. We drove straight back home so Dad could pick up his mountain gear, then he went out looking for you. I stayed at the rescue base, in case you came back down yourself or the search party found you.'

'Do you think Dad will be OK now?'

'Eventually,' she said. 'Don't expect miracles. It's going to take time. Maybe a very long time. He's going to talk to the counsellor later this week. It's a start.'

'Yes,' he said. 'A start. Where's Mark? Is he...?'

Alive, alive. He couldn't say the word.

'Mark will be fine,' she said. 'He's got concussion too, and a few broken bones. He'll have to stay in hospital for a while but he should make a full recovery. Callie's with him now.' She paused. 'I spoke to Grandpa Cullen earlier.'

'Spoke to him? How?'

She laughed. 'The same way I'm speaking to you, numbskull. He's been ill. He's not dead. Anyway, Callie might come and stay with us for a few weeks, just until things are sorted out. Is that all right with you?'

'Yeah,' he said. 'Of course it is. What about Mark? What will happen to him?'

'He'll be in hospital for a couple of weeks. They're going to discharge Grandpa Cullen in a few days' time, so he'll be back home by the time Mark comes out. Mark will probably move back in with him, for a while anyway.'

'That woman, Mrs Hopkinson, said Grandpa Cullen was dying.'

'Well, he could have died, I suppose. But he's had surgery and he's well on his way to a full recovery. Dad and I will help out as much as we can with Mark, and Mrs Hopkinson will too. They'll be OK.'

'We're going to be all right, aren't we, Mum?'

'Yes, we're going to be all right.'

'Can we go and see Mark and Callie now?'

'You've only just woken up.'

'Yeah, I know.'

'Don't you want some breakfast first? There's a tray here with delicious cold toast and a pot of strawberry yoghurt.'

'I'm not hungry.'

'You should eat something. You need to get your strength up.'

'The yoghurt then. I'll pass on the cold toast.'

She watched as he ate, then she stood up. 'I brought you a change of clothes from home. They're at the end of your bed. Can you manage by yourself?'

He grinned. 'I've been dressing myself for years now.'

'Smart aleck.'

She drew the curtains around his bed and waited as he got changed. It took him a long time. His muscles were so stiff he had to hold on to the bed as he pushed one leg and then the other into his jeans.

He came out through the curtains, smiled at Mum. 'OK, I'm ready.'

She put her arm around his waist and steered him towards the double doors.

THIRTY~SIX

They walked slowly along the corridor. Past doors that led to other rooms and wards. They walked through a throng of anxious visitors and busy nurses and patients swinging along on crutches. They went through a set of double doors into a corridor with a mural of a deep dark forest painted along the length of both walls. They passed a wolf and a raven and a moonlit waterfall and an owl with great golden eyes. They went through a blue door into a room with just one bed in it.

Callie was sitting at the bedside. Mark was lying on his back. One leg splinted and hoisted. His shoulder in a cast, his head bandaged, his eyes closed. He looked smaller, frailer. A tube from a drip-bag fed into a vein on his forearm. Wires. A monitor of some sort.

Ash stared down at him. Best friend. Enemy. The boy who'd tried to kill him. The boy who'd tried to save him.

The boy he'd saved.

'Has he woken up at all yet?' said Mum.

Callie was watching Mark. She didn't look round. 'Yes, about an hour ago,' she said. 'The nurses came and checked him. He's just sleeping now.'

Mum touched Ash's arm. 'I'm going to make a few phone calls, give you a bit of time to yourselves. I'll be back in about twenty minutes. OK?'

'OK.'

Ash stood in the doorway. 'How's he doing?'

Callie didn't answer. Her gaze never left Mark.

'Mum says he'll be all right,' Ash said. 'The doctors told her.'

Callie looked at him then. Her fragile bony face. Eyes huge with tiredness and worry. 'He's not all right,' she said. 'He's alive but he's not all right.'

'He'll be home before too long, Mum says.'

'We haven't got a home.'

He didn't answer. There was another chair by the window. He sat in it, glanced outside across the tops of tall pine trees where rooks flapped and tumbled in the wind.

'You look tired,' he said. 'Did you get any sleep last night?'

She shook her head.

'Mum says you can stay with us,' he said. 'You know, until things are sorted out.'

'What's going to be sorted out? Who's going to sort it?'

He shrugged. 'I don't know. Your grandpa, I suppose. Have you seen him yet?'

'Yes. They brought him down to visit Mark last night. He's a lot better.'

'Mum thinks Mark will move back in with him.'

Silence. Her gaze steady on Mark.

At last she said, 'What happened up there?'

'He caught up with me on Stag's Leap. We fought and we got too close to the edge.'

'Did he try to kill you?'

The question was so raw it shocked him. 'It started out like that,' he said. 'Yeah. He kept slamming into me, trying to push me off the Leap. He nearly succeeded. Then he stopped, right at the edge. When it came down to it, he couldn't go through with it.'

'What happened then? How did you fall?'

'We got too close to the edge, that's all. The wind was so strong up there and rain was hammering down and the ghost boys were mobbing us. I lost my footing. Mark tried to save me. He grabbed my wrist and tried to pull me back, away from the edge, but I was already falling so he fell with me.'

'I'm sorry,' she said. 'All that stuff he was talking about, blood for blood and life for life. It scared me but I never thought he'd actually go through with it.'

'He didn't go through with it,' said Ash. 'In the end, he didn't. You were right. He's not a killer. He's just messed up. I don't think most of it was his doing anyway.'

'What do you mean?'

'Those ghost hound boys. They hunt the stag boy every year, only most years they're weak, just so much mountain mist. This year they were strong though. The foot-and-mouth, the slaughter, the drought, your dad killing himself, all that sort of amplified them, made them stronger. They fed off all that somehow. It made them strong enough to kill and they nearly did kill me, and Mark too. We were lucky, that's all.'

'Not just lucky,' she said. 'You saved Mark's life. You could have just waited on the ledge until the search party found you and Mark would probably have died. But instead you risked your life and you climbed up, went to get help.'

'Yeah, well. I couldn't just let him die out there.'

'You saved his life. You and your dad.'

Ash looked away, embarrassed.

'Do you think it's over now?' said Callie.

Ash gazed out of the window again. The grey sky, the pine trees jagged and black against it.

'Yeah, I think so. The hounds are back where they belong. The rain came. The drought's over and the wildfire's probably burnt out by now. The land will heal.'

In the bed, Mark moved, cried out in his sleep.

They stared at him.

His eyelids flickered. His eyes half opened.

He looked at them for a long time. Then he whispered something, his voice so weak that they couldn't make out the words.

Callie took Mark's hand in hers. They sat with him, said nothing.

He was asleep again by the time Mum came back.

'How's Mark doing now?' she asked.

'He woke up,' said Ash. 'Not for long though.'

'Best leave him to rest now,' said Mum. 'I'm going to take you home. You too, Callie. We'll come back tomorrow, during visiting hours.'

'I want to stay with Mark,' said Callie.

But Mum shook her head. 'You need something to eat and a hot bath and a good night's rest. Mark's in good hands. The best thing you can do for him right now is take care of yourself.'

Ash expected Callie to argue, for all that stubborn fire inside her to blaze out. But instead she just nodded, stood up. In her torn and muddy dress, her dark hair still wind-knotted, she looked like a lost child.

'Home it is then,' said Mum.

THIRTY~SEVEN

The spare room where Dad had been sleeping. Curtains and window open and sunlight pouring in. All the junk gone, removed to the garage. A red rug on the floor, the bed made up with clean sheets, a duvet.

Callie stood in the doorway, watching Dad angle a little bedside table into place.

Dad looked rough but he smiled at her. 'Will this do for you?' he said.

Callie nodded, solemn and silent.

'Tomorrow we're going to visit your grandpa in hospital and arrange to pick up your things from his house,' said Dad. 'You'll feel more at home when you've got your own things around you.'

Outside the window, a rook alighted on a branch of the old apple tree and preened its feathers in the soft light.

Dad and Callie watched the bird and Ash watched them and thought how they were both broken but both still standing, sometimes faltering, falling, yet getting up again, keeping going.

He left them there, went outside and sat on the bench at the front of the house. Dark clouds rolling over Tolley Carn. Beyond it, blackened slopes where the wildfire had burned itself out. Here and there, faint scarves of smoke trailed where the land still smouldered.

A rook winging past.

Where were they now, the ghostly stag boy, the hounds, the wolf?

Bone Jack's voice in his head.

Back where they belong, it said. *Back where it's quiet, where they can rest.*

Mark, smashed and hollowed out, his summer burn faded under the stark hospital lights.

Ash stood in the corridor, watching him through the glass pane in the door.

'Are you going in?' said Dad. 'Don't be too long. He's still in a bad way.'

'Dad, I don't know what to say to him. What should I say to him?'

'Just say the first thing that comes into your mind,' said Dad.

Ash nodded, drew a deep breath and went into Mark's room.

'Why didn't you kill me?' he said.

The wind keened at the window. Grey sky, a slash of rain glittering on the glass.

The summer over.

Mark still strapped into casts, his eyes closed, tears silvering his cheeks.

'Why didn't you kill me? Why did you change your mind?'

Nothing.

'I need to know.'

'I almost did kill you,' said Mark.

'I know. Then you stopped and tried to save me. Why?'

'Because of what you said about my dad saving your dad's life up there. Because you were alive, and you wanted to live.'

Ash shook his head. Not good enough. 'What does that mean? I don't know what that means.'

A long silence, then Mark started to talk. 'You know when my mum died? We were friends so you know all about it. It was a long time ago. Half my life. But I remember it like it only just happened. I remember all of it. It was like part of my dad died too, when Mum did. Like we lost them both. He hardly ever smiled after that. He just worked. All the time, working. And then last year there was foot-and-mouth and I was out there for hours with him, day after day, bringing our sheep down from the mountains, watching the government men kill them, watching them burn. He couldn't take it. Then he hung himself.'

'And you found him. Callie told me.'

'She doesn't know everything. I didn't tell her everything.'

'Didn't tell her what?'

'That he was still alive when I went into the barn. He was up there in the hayloft, where you and I used to mess around. He'd already tied the rope to a rafter. He already had the noose round his neck. And I went in and I guess I yelled or something because he looked straight at me. Straight at me, Ash. And then he jumped anyway.'

Ash couldn't breathe, couldn't speak. In his mind's eye he saw it all. The barn at night, Mark going in, looking up. And Tom Cullen, his expression cold and faraway, already out of reach. Then falling through the darkness.

The crack of his neck breaking.

'It's OK,' said Ash softly. 'You don't need to tell me any more.'

And there was no need. He knew it all now. How Mark couldn't get his dad's death out of his head. How he'd tried to erase it, make his dad's death unhappen. How everything had got jumbled up in the madness of his grief: the folk tales his dad and grandpa used to tell, the Stag Chase, the ghostly hound boys drawn to his pain, no more than breaths of mist at first but growing stronger all the time. Mark had come to believe that if he killed the stag boy, he could bring his dad back from the dead. Life for life.

But in the end, Mark had chosen life and the living over the dead.

'What happens now?' said Mark.

'You'll go stay with your grandpa when you get out of hospital. Then we just get on with it, I suppose,' said Ash. 'One foot forward, then the other.'

Mark gave a weak smile. 'So cheesy.'

'I know,' said Ash. 'It works though. You should try it. You just keep going until you get to where you need to be. That's how we got you down off the mountain.'

'I don't remember any of that,' said Mark. 'I remember trying to push you off the Leap. There was this look in your eyes, like you still couldn't believe I'd really go through with it, even though you were inches from the edge. You still trusted me somehow. Then you told me about how my dad saved your dad and suddenly it was like I was standing outside myself, watching this crazy person trying to kill you, only the crazy person was me. And I knew my dad wouldn't want that, no way, and I kind of froze. I couldn't do it. But the ghost hounds rushed us and you lost your balance and I lunged and grabbed you but we both fell. I remember going over the edge, and after that I don't remember anything until I woke up here. I don't even know how you climbed up from that ledge we fell on to.'

'It was the stag boy,' said Ash. 'The ghost stag boy. They must have hunted him up there, centuries ago, and he fell off the Leap and landed on that ledge, and he climbed up. He showed me how to do it. He survived and so did we.'

Tears glittering on Mark's cheeks again. 'I'm sorry,' he said. 'I'm so sorry.'

'It's OK,' said Ash. 'We made it. We both made it home.'

A knock at the door. Dad came in. 'You ready?'

'Yeah,' said Ash. He stood up, looked at Mark. 'I'll come back tomorrow, if you like.'

Mark smiled. 'Yeah. That would be good.'

THIRTY~EIGHT

Early November. The leaves on the beech trees like copper shields. The nights drawing in and the mountains ghostly with low cloud. Soon there would be snow on the high peaks, ice cracking underfoot.

One day he found Callie in the garden, crouched. In her cupped hands, a tiny brown bird, loose with death. Its eye was still gleaming, a bead of bright blood on its beak.

'It flew into the window,' she said, and sobs shook through her.

He touched her shoulder, turned away, went back inside the house.

There were no races he could run for her, no trophies he could lay at her feet.

There was only damage that would take a long time to heal.

From his bed, he watched the trees move in the wind.

He thought about Callie, and the bird. He thought about Mark, the stag boy, Bone Jack.

It still wasn't over. Not yet.

Next day he walked up the lane, past winter-black trees and silent fields, along the old drovers' paths through the mountains to Corbie Tor.

In the valley below, the sluggish stream of summer was now a little rushing river, sparking in the late-morning sunlight. The autumn winds had stripped most of the leaves from the thorn trees. Heavy clusters of haws the colour of dried blood hung among their dark boughs.

He went down, jumped rock to rock across the river, pushed his way through the thorn trees to the bothy with its grimy windows and the bone strings rattling in the doorway.

A rook flapped down and settled on a branch. Then another, and another. They shook out their feathers and filled the air with their rough cries. He waited, half expecting Bone Jack to appear through the trees, but Bone Jack didn't come.

Ash stood outside the doorway in a drift of dead leaves. He hesitated. Then he stepped inside.

No one there. Everything was as he remembered it: the fox skull on the shelf, the old army knife, the flint arrowheads. The book.

The book he'd taken last time he came, the old copy of *The Battle of the Trees* that the wind had ripped apart in his hands. Only now it was intact once more, and back where he'd found it.

> *I have been in a multitude of shapes,*
> *Before I assumed a consistent form...*

He closed the book and went outside.

The autumn sun low over the mountains.

The mew of a buzzard.

A cold wind blowing.

Ash ran. Ran past Corbie Tor and along the high paths and soon a shadow ran with him, a shadow that became a clay-daubed boy with a great wolf racing at his side. And Ash and the stag boy ran and laughed for the joy of it, for the wildness of it, for the fierce beauty of the wolf and for the story of the land that had not yet ended, that would never end.

Acknowledgements and Author's Note

Special thanks go to my agent Joanna Swainson, my editors Eloise Wilson, Charlie Sheppard, and Ruth Knowles.

The lines from *Cad Goddeu (The Battle of the Trees)* used in *Bone Jack* are taken from William F. Skene's translation in *The Four Ancient Books of Wales* (1868).

The Cry of the Wolf

MELVIN BURGESS

'A writer of the highest quality with exceptional powers of insight.'
Sunday Times

It was a mistake for Ben to tell the Hunter that there are still wolves in Surrey. For the Hunter is a fanatic, always on the lookout for unusual prey. Driven by an ambition to wipe out the last English wolves, the Hunter sets out on a savage quest. But what happens when the Hunter becomes the hunted?

'A disturbing book, but of real quality; you will applaud the end.'
Observer

'A Dickens of the future.'
Michael Rosen

9781849393751 £5.99